# REASON TO DIE

# DEBBIE DE LOUISE

Cover Art

Kelly L. Abell/ Select-O-Grafix

http://selectografix.com/

Publisher's Note:

This is a work of fiction. All names, characters, places, and events are the work of the author's imagination.

Any resemblance to real persons, places, or events is coincidental.

Solstice Publishing - www.solsticepublishing.com

# Reason to Die

# By Debbie De Louise

To my husband, Anthony, who has never let his handicap
get in the way of his life.

# Prologue

Chirpy sat in his cage. She could hear his feathers brushing against the bars as he moved around looking for a spot to perch. Otherwise, he was unusually quiet. It bothered her because she enjoyed the parrot's chatter. It covered the sounds of the house, the creaks and groans that woke her at night. The footsteps that haunted her dreams. It was her own fault, Agnes reflected as she sat in the rocker reading the braille books the nice man from the Helen Keller Center brought to her door yesterday. It was great that they had such a program for the blind. Before she lost her sight, she was an avid reader. Now she could still enjoy the written word.

After the burglary last year, Edna had wanted her to move in with her, but what would two old sisters who had nothing in common do with one another all day? Just because Agnes was blind didn't mean she couldn't take care of herself. She placed her book on the floor by the rocker and eased herself off the chair using the cane propped next to it. She'd gotten quite adept at maneuvering through the small house, knew every corner, the edges of every piece of furniture. She was able to cook, iron her clothes, clean Chirpy's cage, and feed him. She didn't need or want another Seeing Eye dog even though Edna said one would be good protection, and her own doctor suggested it would give her a reason to get out of the house. But she was fine with the bird, been fine with him for nine years since Smoky, her German Shepherd, passed away. She wasn't completely sightless. She could see gray shadows and even some large objects, but nothing was clear. It didn't matter. She was seventy-five years old and had been legally blind most of her life.

She was just ten when the accident happened. Edna, her older sister, still seemed to have some guilt about it, but it was Agnes' own fault. She loved science as a child and the experiment seemed like fun until the chemicals exploded into her face. Her parents were out, and Edna was babysitting but talking on the phone with her boyfriend at the time. Not the small cell gadgets, like they have today, but a rotary dial phone. She remembered her twisting the cord around as she spoke, giggling. When Agnes went into the bathroom to mix the concoction, Edna was three rooms away.

As Agnes walked to the bathroom now, she tapped her cane around in habit. She knew the twenty steps down the hall by heart. She had her own built-in GPS. But the cane was a comfort, a guide she hesitated to give up.

When she was through taking care of her needs, she started back to the living room. Chirpy suddenly began squawking. She thought he was resting. Something had stirred him. Then she heard a noise by the front door. Someone was on her step.

"Settle down, Chirpy. Looks like we have a visitor," she said as she cut across the room to answer the light knock. The bird continued to squawk. She wondered why he was so excited.

"Who is it?" she called when she got to the door.

A male voice replied, "Talking Books delivery for Ms. McCarver."

How very strange. She'd had a delivery of the audio books last week, and they usually only arrived once a month in a box delivered by the mailman. Maybe there had been a mistake.

"I haven't ordered any new books," she said, "and they usually come in the mail."

"No mistake, Ma'am. Talking books are being hand delivered now. Can you please open the door and take them? I have several more stops to make today."

Agnes hesitated a moment. Chirpy had finally quieted down. Edna would probably scold her for letting a stranger in the house just because he claimed he had audiobooks for her, but he sounded nice enough. He sounded a lot like the kind librarian from the Helen Keller Library who visited yesterday.

Reaching up, she unlatched the safety lock and then twisted the doorknob. She heard the man step forward. He closed the door behind him and then pushed her to the ground. Her cane flew away. She tried to grab for it, but it was out of reach. It happened so fast, a scream lodged in her throat as he put his gloved hands around it and squeezed. From a hazy distance of fear, she heard Chirpy start squawking again. The pressure on her throat tightened. She couldn't yell or even talk. Blackness engulfed her as the gray shadows of her limited sight dissolved. All she could hear in those last moments were Chirpy crashing against his bars in a useless attempt to free himself and the bad man's raspy breathing against her cheek as he squeezed the life out of her. He spoke one last time, but his voice was no longer kind. It was cruel and heartless. "Tell me, Ms. McCarver, do you have a reason to live?"

As she fell into unconsciousness, she wondered why he'd asked such a strange question when he knew she would not be able to respond.

# Chapter One

Courtney looked up from her paperwork when Mark entered the office. "Visitor," the bird announced. He had quite the vocabulary for a parrot. Her heart sank at the thought that he'd lost his owner so tragically.

"Hey there, beautiful," her partner said, approaching her desk. "You bogged down on the blind woman's case? Decided what to do with her bird yet?"

She shook her head and then ran a hand through her blonde bangs to feather them back. "Yes and No. I thought about giving him to Bill, but I know he won't accept him."

"Why don't you take him?"

"I wish I could, but I can't with Oliver. Cats and birds don't mix well, even if he stays in his cage."

"Maybe the Captain will let you keep him here as the Baxter PD mascot?"

She laughed. "You kidding? Sansone would never do that."

"I could take him to my place. You're there often enough to help me take care of him. I've never had a bird."

"Let me think about it." She paused, looking down at the file in front of her. "Back to the case. I did find something strange, but I almost hoped the bird could tell me what really happened."

Mark took a seat next to her desk, his long legs stretched out, ankles crossed. As partners, they shared an office that was more of a cubicle than an actual room. "What's that, Detective?"

"I thought this woman looked familiar." She passed him the crime scene photo of Agnes McCarver. It wasn't a pretty sight. The elderly woman had been strangled in her home. "Bill and I met her last year when her house was burgled, and the savings she kept hidden in her pillow were taken."

Mark cringed a bit at the picture and raised a dark eyebrow. "You sure?" She could tell he wasn't happy with the reference to when she worked with another partner, especially one whom she'd dated before him.

"Speak of the devil, here he comes," Mark said.

Courtney glanced to her office door as Bill Thompson wheeled himself in. It always tugged at her heart when she saw him in the chair.

"Good afternoon, Detective Lang, Detective Farrell." He greeted them with half a smile. She hadn't seen a full smile on his face since that awful day he'd been shot and crippled.

"Hi, Bill. Why the formality?"

"Would you rather I call you—idiot?"

That widened the smile to almost three-quarters across his stubbled cheek.

Mark rose, and Courtney couldn't help but think he was challenging Bill by showing off his height. At 6'5, he was way taller than Bill, even if he'd been able to stand.

"I was just about to leave. I need to check some things in Evidence. By the way, I'm thinking of taking the bird. Courtney wanted to give it to you, but she said you wouldn't be interested."

The smile disappeared completely as the men locked eyes. "She's right. I can't take care of myself—how can I care for a pet?"

"Still attending that pity party, I see." Mark went to the door and looked back at his partner. "Talk to you later, Courtney. Good luck."

When Mark was gone, Courtney turned her gaze on Bill. She still found it hard to look directly into his deep brown eyes because the pain was still there, masked by anger, but she forced herself to talk to him and not at him.

Disabled people hated stares, but they appreciated manners. "Sorry. That was awkward. You're still jealous of him?"

Bill sighed and looked away. "I have no reason to be jealous. You forget I'm the one who broke it off, Detective Lang."

"Back to formalities. Okay, you're right, Detective Thompson. You didn't think I could cope with a man who couldn't walk. But that doesn't mean you aren't jealous of Mark, uh, Detective Farrell."

"No, if anyone's jealous, it's him. Why, I have no idea. He can't possibly think we'd get back together."

"Maybe he does. Look, Bill, and sorry I'm making this casual, but if we're going to keep working together— the three of us, this can't continue. Now what did you want to see me about?"

Bill glanced at the parrot who was preening himself, his green-yellow feathers spread. She was surprised he wasn't talking, but she had a feeling he was listening.

"You told me you had some research you wanted me to do regarding the McCarver murder. I take it you notified the sister?"

"She's the one who found her. She was questioned but not very coherent at the time. I'll be talking with her later today." Speaking with Edna Black would not be easy, but it would probably be way easier than talking to Bill after he'd been released from the hospital six months ago.

"So, what exactly do you want me to check? I have loads of time and nothing to do but browse social media on the PD's PC."

Courtney knew Bill hated being confined to the desk after having served with her in the field. She was relieved, though, that he was sticking with the job. She feared he would give up and accept the generous offer of disability pay compensation for an officer injured in the line of duty. Instead, he insisted on staying. She had to give him credit for that.

"I need you to dig up the file on the break-in and robbery at Ms. McCarver's house last year. The one we worked on, remember?" She hated having to bring up their past partnership.

"Sure. I remember." His voice was flat as he turned the wheelchair around and headed for the door. She was about to open it for him, but he managed it himself. As he slid out into the hall, he called back to her, "I'll get that to you asap, Detective Lang."

She turned back to her paperwork trying to forgive Bill his attitude, but it hurt.

"Sorry," the bird said from his cage. How did he know?

***

Edna Black lived only a few blocks from her sister in a similar ranch house. This one had an evergreen bush outside that was tipped with snow and a few strands of icicle lights. A Santa Claus mat lay at the front door still spreading its holiday welcome despite the fact Christmas had passed weeks ago. Courtney had brought Mark along for the questioning. She needed her partner's support for the task she dreaded. He had been quiet on the ride there, not mentioning Bill or the murder. When they'd pulled up at the house in the squad car, he simply followed her wordlessly to the door. She knew he realized nothing he said would make the job they were about to do any easier.

The small, eighty-year old woman answered the door after looking at them through the peephole even though Courtney had identified them as "Police" after ringing the bell.

Edna's eyes were red-rimmed from crying, and she choked on her words as she invited them to enter. Courtney was surprised she was alone. It seemed the two sisters were the only family one another had. It made it harder.

"Please have a seat," Edna said, leading them into a small living room that was darkened by closed blinds despite the sunny January day they'd walked in from. "I can get some tea if you'd like."

"No, thank you. Please don't go to any trouble."

Although they remained standing, Edna collapsed into a large wing chair that reminded Courtney of one her grandmother used to have. The tiny woman with the white hair also bore a slight resemblance to Grandma Lily who died six months ago, just a week after the night Bill was shot. She pushed away both painful memories as she drew in a breath and began her questions. "I know this is a hard time, Ms. Black, but there are a few things we need to ask you. I'm Detective Lang and this is Detective Farrell." She wanted so badly to hug the little lady, but she had to keep her distance, her professional manner.

"I understand. Thank you for coming." Edna's voice sounded stronger, but her wrinkled hands clenched a handkerchief in her lap.

"Can you please tell us what happened when you visited your sister this morning? The report stated that you found her on the living room floor."

Edna lowered her eyes and took a breath. She seemed fragile, but Courtney had a feeling she was stronger than she looked. "That's right, Detective. She was dead on her back. Her face was blue. That burglar must've done it. I told her to come live here with me. Since Walter died, I've been all alone. There's plenty of room. I don't understand." She sniffled into her hanky and began speaking of her sister in present tense. "Agnes is so stubborn. She's blind, for Pete's sake. All she has is that bird. What protection is that? I'm her sister. Our parents are long gone." She sniffled again, her head still down. "That's all I know. I was on the phone. She was playing with her science kit in the bathroom."

"Excuse us," Mark said drawing the woman back to the present. "The report said you found her in the living room, not the bathroom."

It was as if Edna hadn't heard him. She continued her story. "No, she was in the bathroom screaming. I heard this loud noise and rushed in there. There was acid all over her face. I didn't know what to do." Her words came rapidly, and her blue pupils, lined with spider veins, opened wide. Courtney could see the broken blood vessels in them. "Mama wasn't home. I called 911. I did the right thing, didn't I?"

"Yes," Courtney agreed. The 911 call had come in at 11 a.m. that morning. The officers who had arrived five minutes later had found Edna on the floor cradling her dead sister.

"It was all my fault, wasn't it? I should've been there." Her sobs grew stronger, and her shoulders quaked with the effort.

"It's okay, Ms. Black. You did everything you could."

"No!" she yelled, her tears momentarily stopping. "I was the older sister. Mama told me to take care of her. Our father was dead. Mama had to work, and I had to watch Aggie. I didn't do my job. I killed her." The tears let loose in a stream. Mark grabbed a box of tissues he saw on the side table and brought them to her. They were both familiar with the stages of grief, and it was obvious Edna was facing the guilt one.

They stayed only a few minutes longer because it was cruel to try to get more out of the woman. Courtney gave her a card for a grief counselor and promised to check up on her. She meant to do that.

"One more thing, Officers," Edna said as she led them to the door.

Courtney wondered if she remembered something, but it wasn't about the murder. "Where is Chirpy, my sister's bird?"

"He's at the police station, Ms. Black. He's safe," Courtney assured her.

"I don't have any pets. I had a cat. She died, and I couldn't get another, but I'd like to take Chirpy. May I? Please?"

Courtney glanced at Mark. "Of course, Ms. Black. We'll make sure someone brings him to you."

"Thank you. Walter and I never had children, but I would've loved to have had a son or a daughter like you two. Your parents must be so proud."

\*\*\*

When Courtney and Mark were in the cruiser driving back to the station, she said, "Looks like you're out of a bird."

Mark grinned. "Rats! I'm so disappointed."

"I feel so bad for her."

"You have a soft heart. That's not good in this profession."

"What did you find in Evidence?" She needed to change the subject away from the old woman.

"Nothing that gave us any clues. Do you think she's right about the burglar from last year coming back?"

"I doubt it, although I'm having Bill pull that report. If the guy wanted her dead, he would've killed her when he broke in last time."

"Maybe, but it's the only lead we have right now."

Courtney had to agree he was right.

# Chapter Two

Back at the station, Mark told Courtney he would make another round examining the evidence from both crimes against Mrs. McCarver and then promised to drop off Chirpy with his new owner. She was a little sorry to see the bird leave. When she returned to her office, she fed him some of the birdseed they'd taken from Agnes' house.

"Yummy," Chirpy said as his beak pecked the seed.

"You're a funny bird. You'll make Edna feel better. I know Oliver does that when I'm sad."

"Talking to your feathered friend?" Courtney hadn't even heard the squeak of Bill's wheelchair as he entered.

"I just got back from the sister's house, and she's taking him."

"That's nice." Bill had a folder on his lap. He brought it over and placed it on her desk. "The burglary file. Not much in it. They never caught the perp, but you know that."

Courtney fingered the pages, scanning a few lines of each. "I'm just wondering. Do you think there might be a connection between last year's burglaries and those muggings in the park?" When she glanced up after asking the question, she almost wanted to take it back. How could she have forgotten that one of the muggings had cost Bill his mobility?

"I'm sorry . . . I didn't mean..."

He waved his hand, although the expression on his face remained solemn. "I hate it when you tiptoe around me more than I hate when you accuse me of self-pity, Courtney."

"That was Mark, Bill, but I tend to agree with him. When you came back here, I was proud of you, but the way you act around us now . . ."

"Maybe you should seek a transfer, or I could talk to Sansone about one for myself. It's obvious we can't work together anymore."

"That's not true, Bill. You're sensitive, and I can understand that, but this seems to go deeper. Can't we call a truce for now?"

He paused, and she could hear her heart beating in the stillness. Then he lifted his dark eyes and looked into hers. "Sure. I apologize for my behavior. The only connection we ever found between the burglaries and the muggings, besides the fact that money was the objects of both crimes, was that they happened around the same time and the responsible parties were never identified."

"Maybe we should speak to Sansone about reopening those cases."

"What? You can't be serious, Court. There were no valuables or cash taken from McCarver's house, was there?"

"No, but . . ."

"Then I can't see how these crimes are related."

She threw up her hands, dumping the file folder on her desk. "I don't understand, Bill. You, of all people, should want those past crimes solved. This could be a lead. We might be able to find the man who shot you."

"Please, Courtney. Don't go there. I've accepted what happened that night. It hasn't been easy, but I've made peace. I don't want to go through it all over again."

Although she knew in her heart that Bill had far from come to terms with his situation, she decided not to pursue the topic, at least not with him.

"Okay. I'll consider this an isolated incident and treat it as a single crime. Why someone would kill an old blind woman and not even take a cent from her home is beyond me."

"Crazy people do crazy things." He took the file back and made a 360-degree turn with his wheelchair, swinging around so fast, it almost toppled over.

"Watch out, Bill. Let me help you with the door."

Despite his stubbornness, he allowed her to hold it open as he glided through it. She went back to Chirpy, who had finished his meal.

"Mark's taking you to your new home. So, it's bye, bye, birdie, I guess." She laughed at her own joke.

"Bye, bye," Chirpy screeched back as she sat at her desk and put her head in her hands, thinking back to last summer.

***

She heard the whistling and knew immediately who was at the door before the bell rang. When she opened it on Bill's wide smile and saw the roses he was holding, it made her feel so much better after the talking down Sansone gave her earlier that day.

"For my beautiful partner." Bill handed her the roses.

"How sweet. Thank you. Come on in. I wasn't expecting you. Why didn't you call?"

"Sorry. You made a comment once that I wasn't spontaneous enough, so I thought I'd surprise you, and I have another surprise. Put those in water and then come on out. I want to take you somewhere."

She looked down at her jeans. "If we're going anywhere nice, I need to change. I was just about to get into my pajamas. It's nearly eleven o'clock."

He raised a dark eyebrow. "You tempt me speaking about going to bed, but nope. You're perfect the way you're dressed. We're just going for a ride." The smile was still plastered on his face which made her wonder what he was up to. In the year since they'd been dating, she could always tell when he wasn't being honest with her. That's one of the things she loved about him. Now she had a feeling this was more than just a way to cheer her up from her fight with their captain.

"Alright. I'll just be a minute then. Wait for me on the couch." After she'd run water over the stems of the flowers, clipped them, and arranged them in a vase, she quickly brushed out her hair in the bathroom and added an extra dap of lipstick.

When she returned to the living room, Bill was still whistling.

"You seem happier than usual." Bill was always the one to brighten up the police station with his funny yet corny jokes, his off-key singing, and other antics that even brought an occasional laugh out of serious Sansone.

"I'm a happy guy, that's all. Why shouldn't I be? I have you and a great career. I catch criminals and make them wet their pants."

"Bill!" She grabbed his hand and pulled him up. "Before you go any further with the crude comments, let's get going."

Standing next to her, he suddenly embraced her and whispered, "I almost wish we had time for a quickie, but I'm really eager to show you something. We can grab a snack on our way back and eat it in your wonderful bed."

Although she had no idea what he was up to so late at night, she followed him when he released her and walked to the door.

The night was balmy, a perfect late July evening. As Bill drove, she saw a few stars, like diamonds against the dark backdrop of the sky. Since they weren't on duty, he was using his own car. She noticed he wasn't playing any music and seemed more talkative than usual.

"I hate to bring up this afternoon, Court, because I want this to be an extra special night for you, but I'm sorry about what happened with Sansone. She has no reason to blame you on the holdup in catching the Park Mugger."

"I know, Bill. She's just upset that we may have to close the case without solving it. Thanks for your support with the flowers. They really did cheer me up."

"That's not why I brought them." He turned on to the street that led to the park.

"Are we going to the park?"

He grinned. "I wanted to find a nice spot. The mugger hasn't been around in a few weeks now."

Something in the way he sounded made her question why he was looking for a special place. "What's the big secret? What did you want to show me that you needed to bring me to what's been a crime scene over the last few months?"

"I didn't want you to think of it like that. We've had some good times in the park." As he pulled through the gate, he waved to the attendant in the booth.

"Hey, Harry. Just stopping by for a few minutes with Courtney. Glad you're still open."

"Hi, Bill. We're closing in a half hour. It's been quiet so far. Are you two on undercover patrol?"

"No, just taking a drive in the park."

Harry nodded. "Nice night for it. Clear skies, and did you see that moon?"

"Sure did. It's beautiful like my girl here."

Courtney felt a blush heat her cheeks. Bill pulled away and circled the park. After a few minutes, he turned into a parking spot near the gazebo. The area was empty.

"I'm surprised there are no police around and that they still keep the place open this late."

"This isn't where the mugger usually strikes, Courtney, and Harry would stop anyone entering if they looked suspicious."

"There are side streets into the park. Someone could walk in."

"Stop being so pessimistic. Tonight is a night of magic."

"What are you up to?"

Bill turned off the car's engine. "I brought you here because I have an important question to ask you." He rolled down his window to let the warm night breeze through. Courtney gazed at the full moon spotlighting the area. Then she saw something brighter in Bill's face, a ray of hope as he took a small box from his pocket.

"We've been seeing one another awhile, Court, and I think you know how I feel about you. I hope you feel the same." As he lifted the lid of the velvet box to reveal the diamond ring inside, her heart beat fast. She had not expected a marriage proposal, but before she could voice a reply, a scream rang out in the distance.

"What the?" Bill placed the box in the glove compartment and unbuckled his seatbelt. "You stay here. I'll check it out. I'll be right back."

"No. I'm coming with you." Courtney was aware that neither of them had their guns with them. "Maybe we should call 911, Bill."

"There isn't time. Let's just go see."

They ran together following the sound. Before they reached where they thought it was coming from, it stopped. Turning the corner of a hedge, they found a woman laying against a large rock. Her head had been bashed in, her purse open on the ground spilling its contents of lipstick, tissues, cell phone and assorted items, but no wallet or cash.

"Check her out, Courtney. I thought I saw someone run over there. Call for backup."

As Bill ran away, Courtney checked the woman's pulse. She was dead. If the park mugger had struck again, this time he had killed his victim.

As she dialed 911, Courtney heard a shot ring out. Holding her phone and speaking in quick breaths, she headed in its direction. Bill was on the ground, bleeding from a wound in his back.

"Oh, my God!" She took off her blazer and tried to staunch the bleeding. "Don't move, Bill. Help is on its way. The victim is already dead. Did you see the shooter?"

Bill squeezed his eyes in pain. "He had a mask on. It's the mugger."

# Chapter Three

Courtney was awakened from the memory by the sound of a throat clearing. She looked up to see Sansone standing in the doorway. The tall captain who Bill used to call a flat-chested sergeant when he still had his sense of humor, did not look happy. "May I come in?"

Chirpy let out a squawk. "Visitor."

"Yes, Captain." She stood and addressed her boss. She noticed how the bird retreated to the back of its cage.

"It has come to my attention that you are investigating the McCarver murder by pulling some old files about the Park Mugger."

Bill had ratted her out. "That's correct, Captain." She wouldn't lie. She had to face the music.

"And why is that?" Sansone raised her pencil-thin eyebrows. Even though her hair was black with strands of gray that framed her angular face, her eyebrows were so light they faded into her sallow skin. Courtney had known her for ten years since she joined the force at twenty-two right out of college. In all that time, the woman hadn't aged but always looked old. She could imagine Natalie Sansone was never a beauty.

"I think the crimes are related." She watched the captain's face pale. She knew how much the unsolved muggings had nagged at her. How Sansone had blamed Courtney for losing one of the best leads they'd had on it. It had taken a toll on their relationship. Not that they'd had anything close to a friendship, but Sansone had once respected Courtney a whole lot more than she did after the Park Mugger's case was closed, after Bill was shot.

"I'm afraid that I don't see any similarities." She stepped back toward the door. "I would hope that you continue to focus on the current crime and stop looking for clues that don't exist. It's quite a change for someone who missed one that was staring her in the face."

Before Courtney could think of a reply, Sansone had stomped back to her office.

"Goodbye," Chirpy said.

"And good riddance," Courtney added softly.

\*\*\*

Heading back home at the end of the day, Courtney was exhausted. She hadn't wanted to allow Sansone's talking down to affect her so much, but it did. What also hurt, strangely, was when Mark picked Chirpy up from her office to take him to Edna. In the short time the bird had occupied the spot by her desk, she'd grown attached to the feathered creature. Even so, the tears that wet her eyes as Mark took the cage surprised her.

"Goodbye," Chirpy squawked.

She waved sadly. "Bye, bye."

"I told you I should've taken him," Mark said, "but maybe Edna will let you visit him."

"I should do that. She seems lonely, especially now that her sister is gone. Even worse, she's guilty and that guilt goes back way further than Agnes' murder."

"What do you mean?"

"You saw how she lapsed back to the childhood incident that blinded her sister. I'm sure she's lived with that memory for years." Courtney knew all about being haunted by the past.

\*\*\*

Courtney opened her door after grabbing the letters stuck in her mailbox. Tossing them on the kitchen table, she gave them a quick glance—bills, ads—nothing urgent. She would deal with them later. She put on the tea kettle, slipped out of her heels, and took a seat on her couch with her stockinged feet propped up. Oliver came from a back room, most likely her bedroom, and joined her.

"Thanks for welcoming me home, boy," she said petting his creamy head. The Siamese looked up at her through his blue eyes and let out a loud meow.

"I know you're hungry. I have to get up for my tea, anyway. Just keep it down, or the neighbors will start complaining."

Courtney lived on a quiet street and kept mostly to herself. The small house she rented was her aunt Violet's who now lived in Florida with her uncle. Oliver had been Violet's cat, but Courtney had "inherited" him" because the senior complex where they moved didn't allow pets. Courtney and Oliver had bonded immediately, and she was thankful for both the home and the cat. She'd moved to Tilly Court from her parents' house after the fire, living with Violent, Vince, and Oliver until her aunt and uncle moved down South two years ago.

Oliver was crying and circling her legs as she changed his water and opened a can of cat food.

"Be patient, Oliver."

As she placed the paper plate of food and his water bowl by his feeding station, a knock sounded at her door.

She didn't have many visitors and hoped it wasn't someone selling something. She wasn't in the mood for that tonight. She just wanted to curl up with Oliver and a good book.

Leaving the cat to his meal, she approached the door. As a cop, her first instinct was to check the peephole. It was dark, but she kept an outside light on until she went to bed. It illuminated Mark's face.

She opened the door. "What are you doing here?"

"Nice greeting, Courtney. I just dropped Chirpy off with Edna and thought I'd come by to spend some time with you. I know you were a bit upset by losing the bird."

She laughed. "C'mon in. I have Oliver, remember? I was looking forward to a quiet night with him."

"Sorry to ruin your plans." He walked in. "I have to admit I have an ulterior motive I'd like to talk to you about."

He sounded serious, but she could never tell. "Well, I have hot water on if you want tea, or I could make some coffee. Why don't you take a seat on the couch?"

"Certainly, but don't go to any trouble. Tea is fine with a touch of sugar, but not that herbal stuff, please."

Oliver was still lapping up his food when Courtney returned to the kitchen. She poured tea for them, added a cube of sugar to Mark's, and then a few biscuits on the tray with their cups.

"Here you go, Detective Farrell." She placed the tray on the oval table in front of the couch. All the furnishings in the house were still her aunt's. Even though Violet said she could replace anything she wanted, Courtney was content with the décor. Her aunt had been an interior decorator, and her taste reflected it.

"Thank you." Mark blew on the tea and then took a sip. "Perfect, and I can definitely use the cookies."

"They're biscuits."

"Sorry. I'm not good with words, as you know. Come sit next to me."

As Courtney joined him, he placed his arm around the top of the couch lightly touching her shoulder. "That's better. I've missed you."

"You see me every day at work."

"You know what I mean." A week ago, they'd had an argument and agreed not to see one another personally again.

Courtney looked down. She hadn't taken anything from the tray. He took her action as a sign of agreement.

"That's why I'm here. I want you to reconsider, but I have a question. Look at me, please." He put down his cup and turned to face her, his hazel eyes gazing into hers when she lifted them.

"Mark . . ."

"Just one question. It's not difficult. You should know the answer immediately."

"Don't interrogate me."

"That's not what this is, Court." He took a breath. "Are you still hung up on Bill? Is that the real reason you broke off with me? Or is it the guilt you feel about what happened to him?"

Courtney hadn't told Mark about Bill proposing before he was shot. No one knew about that except Bill's brother, Rick.

She stood up. "I think you should leave, Mark."

"I had a feeling that would be your response. Thanks for the tea, anyway." As he walked to the door, he looked back over his shoulder and said, "I was right on both counts, I guess."

She didn't reply. She waited until he'd closed the door behind him before she let loose her tears. He'd been right about what he said, but he'd missed one other truth. The main reason she'd stepped away from their relationship before it got too deep was because she feared she would injure him as she had Bill, as she had her mother and younger sister. The people she loved were in danger. There was a curse on her, and those she cared about paid the price.

She went to the bathroom and rinsed her face with cold water. She had to snap out of it. There was no use crying. She was a grown woman, a homicide detective. Her cell phone rang as she was drying her eyes. She ran back to the living room where Oliver occupied the same spot Mark had on the couch, his brown paw batting her phone around.

"Give me that, cat!" She took the "toy" away, ignoring the sad look in his blue eyes.

The display showed Mark's number. She hesitated to answer. Was he calling to apologize? She didn't want that. She was the one who was sorry, but she had no choice in the matter.

"Yes, Mark." Her reply was flat, with as little emotion as she could place behind it.

"Courtney, there's been another one. A deaf man. He's been strangled, too. Sansone is chomping at the bit. They have a name for the killer. They're calling him the Handicapped Strangler."

"Oh, my God! That's not even politically correct. He should be the Disabled Strangler, but that's not even right if he's killing disabled people. Are there any other similarities to McCarver's case?"

"Don't know yet." He gave her the address of the crime scene and asked her to meet him there.

As she tapped the "end call" button, she was mad at herself for feeling better. The new murder had helped because now she could be her professional, all-business self and not think of emotions and personal relationships. She gave Oliver a pat on his head and left the house.

# Chapter Four

When she arrived at the scene, she was surprised it was at dormitory housing even though Mark had given the address of Baxter University.

He was waiting for her by a group of police cars parked behind Craig Hall. Having attended the school more than a decade ago, she knew that all the male dorms had men's names and all the female units were named after women. It got a little quirky telling the difference with all the foreign names and those that were unisex.

"What do you have?" she asked, rushing over to Mark.

"Male student, Joseph Hamilton, Junior year, deaf. His roommate found him. I questioned the guy. He's pretty broken up. He was with his girlfriend tonight at the campus hangout while his buddy was cramming for an exam in the room. When he came back, he found him in bed with a rope around his neck. It wasn't staged to look like a suicide."

"Did anyone see anything? What's the security like in the building?"

He shook his head. "There's always an R.A. at the desk, and ID's are checked when people enter after 11 p.m. Before that, they just use their campus card to swipe the door."

"So, he had a card. That points to a student."

"Maybe, or he could've stolen one. We need to check that out. The R.A. didn't notice anyone strange, but when we spoke to him, his girlfriend was there, and I think he was more preoccupied with her than watching the door."

"Why does Sansone think this is related to McCarver's murder? Just because he was strangled and had a disability?"

"Sansone isn't the one labelling it, but there are rumors going around. Some of the officers like to spread stuff like this. Judge for yourself. He was a young guy, not an old lady, like Ms. McCarver. He didn't live alone but had a roommate who'd been rooming with him since freshman year."

"I'd like to talk to the roommate, if he's up to it."

"Hopefully, he's more composed. Come with me."

Courtney followed Mark into the building. A group of students stood around whispering and gawking. A few cops stood in the hall and outside a room on the first floor where Mark led her.

She recognized Kurt Kelly and nodded at him. "Hello, Officer Kelly. Is the witness coherent?"

"Yes, Detective Lang. He's inside. So is the body and Officer Graham."

Mark stepped aside to allow her to enter through the yellow tape. He stayed outside chatting with Kelly.

The first thing Courtney noticed was how messy the room was, but it hadn't been trashed. It was the typical chaotic appearance of a male dorm room. The witness stood staring out the window as Officer Graham bagged evidence and the M.E. that she knew from previous murders examined the body on the bed.

There were rope burns and marks on the man's throat. His eyes bulged out in panic. Her stomach took a turn, but she couldn't look away.

"He's been dead about three hours," Phillips said. The medical examiner was about Courtney's age but looked years older. Her hair was gray and pulled back. All her features were straight lines. Her face was expressionless. Courtney knew to do this job one had to be hard and dissociative. "Strangled. Graham bagged the rope. Looks like he struggled and was more of a challenge to our killer than McCarver."

"Hey, we haven't determined it's the same person."

"I'd bet my examining gloves on it. Too much of a coincidence, a blind lady and then a deaf kid within a day of one another."

Courtney didn't want to argue with Phillips. She walked over to the man at the window.

"Excuse me, I'm Detective Lang. I know my partner already questioned you, but would you mind answering a few more questions, please?"

The man turned. His eyes and nose were red. He held some tissues in his hand. A day's growth of beard bristled his chin. His eyes were dark and very sad.

"Sure. If it can help. I can't believe this happened to Joe. I'm Steve. Stephen Willis." He held out his shaking hand.

"Nice to meet you, Mr. Willis. I'm sorry it's under these circumstances."

He sniffed. "Me, too."

"I know you found your roommate dead in bed. Was he acting strange at all or did anything happen recently that caused anyone to be mad at him?"

Willis shook his head, his unbrushed curly hair waving from side to side. It reminded her of black poodle fur for some reason. "Nope. Everyone loved Joe. He was a great guy, and you would never know he was handicapped. He was born deaf, but he managed better than most people. He was in honors. I studied sign language, so we could communicate better, but he read lips well. We never had trouble talking. I never felt he was any different than any of my friends."

"So, this must've been a shock to you?"

"Totally." He wiped his eyes with a crumpled tissue.

Courtney didn't see how she could get anything else out of him, and she didn't want to upset him further. "Okay. Thanks for talking with me. We're going to do our best to catch whoever did this."

As she went to join Mark outside, Willis called her back. "Wait. There was something that happened. I forgot to mention it to your partner. It wasn't recent, so I almost forgot about it."

"Go on," Courtney prompted. She took out the pad and pen she always kept tucked inside her jacket–pocket. Mark had been on her to start using her cell phone for notes, but she liked the old-fashioned way of jotting down information.

"Joe was such a great guy, and he never thought of himself as unlucky because he was born with a disability. But, last year, he was attacked on campus. His wallet and cell phone were stolen. They were never recovered."

Courtney paused in her writing. "Last year? What was the date? Do you recall the month? There must've been something about it in the paper."

"It was in March. The clocks had just been turned ahead. I remember that. I also remember reading about it in the student paper. I'm sure it was in the local one, too."

"Thanks, Steve. I mean, Mr. Willis. This could be very helpful."

He smiled weakly. "I hope so. You know, some people have such bad luck."

"Unfortunately, that's very true." She thought of Bill.

Back out in the hall, she looked for Mark, but he was no longer talking with Kelly. The officer was still there standing against the wall checking his cell phone. He noticed her exit the room and said, "Your partner went to speak with the R.A. who was at the desk last night. He's up front. His name is Winchester Palmer. What a name, huh? Poor kid, but I think he's rich. It costs a fortune to attend college these days and live on campus, too."

Courtney didn't have time to chat with Kelly. She met up with Mark by the front desk where he was talking to a lanky young man with a goatee she assumed was Palmer and a blonde co-ed with cut-up jeans and a t-shirt cut way too low.

When Mark saw her, he waved her over. "Winchester, Sally, this is my partner Courtney Lang."

So Mark was on first-name terms with the co-eds. She figured he was trying to make them feel at ease, so they would be comfortable talking with him.

"Nice to meet you, Detective Lang." Palmer extended his hand to her. She shook it briefly. His girlfriend just smiled. If the young man was wealthy, he certainly didn't dress it. He wore a plaid shirt that looked like it came from the Salvation Army and jeans that were practically in rags, but sometimes clothes cost more than they looked. It was hard to tell with today's college fashion trends.

"Nice to meet you," she said. She wasn't going to let him address her by first name, not while he was already showing respect for authority. Despite their outfits, the couple looked law abiding. They didn't seem drunk or high.

"How did things go with Steve?" Palmer asked. "Man, he's all broke up over Joe. I don't blame him. I would freak if I found my roommate dead, and Joe was a great guy. The best. Everybody loved him. He never wanted any of us to treat him special because he was deaf."

Sally let out a sob and grabbed a tissue from the open box on the desk. She blotted her eyes, and her mascara bled around them. "Joe was our friend. I can't believe this would happen to him."

"I'm sorry," Courtney said. She was all too aware that life wasn't fair. "Can either of you take us to the student newspaper office? Do you know if they keep old issues here anywhere?"

"I'm the features editor on the paper," Sally said. "I can get security to open the student union building and the office. We keep back issues in the newsroom, and there's an online archive, too."

"Wonderful. Can you do that and take us there?"

Mark turned a curious look on her. While Sally spoke to one of the Baxter security guards who was also being questioned by an officer, Courtney explained about the incident Steve had related to her.

"Another similarity to McCarver."

"How so?"

"They were both victims of previous crimes."

"Could be a coincidence." But that's not what Courtney was thinking. Baxter was not a large town, and the park wasn't far from the college.

"You folks want to go to the *Beacon* office?" The elderly campus guard who addressed them could've been a grandfather to the students.

"Yes, please."

She, Mark, and Sally followed the man from the building and across campus. Sally had whispered in Winchester's ear before she left. He told her he wanted to stay and see if he could be of any help to Steve.

The office of the *Beacon* was on the top floor of the student union building. The security guard, who introduced himself as Max, unlocked the main door and switched on the lights. It was eerily quiet but still retained a strange mixture of odors—fried food, perfume, sweat, and a trace of tobacco and possibly pot, although neither was allowed on campus.

They passed the campus bookstore, a gift shop selling tees and sweatshirts (she even noticed some ripped jeans there) and a Starbucks and Subway. "Boy, college has changed since we were here," Mark whispered to her as they climbed the stairs.

"You attended Baxter?"

"Graduated in 2002. You?"

"2007. They already had most of these here at that time. I see some changes, though."

They entered the newsroom. The guard stood outside. The beige walls were framed with copies of front-page stories and journalism awards. Bins holding papers were stacked around the room. Courtney smelled the scent of newsprint and again a slight whiff of tobacco and pot. A PC stood on a desk in the corner next to a black leather couch.

Courtney surveyed the labels under the open paper bins. They were dated with the most recent issue in front and then went back in time.

"There's five years' worth here. The others are in archives in the library," Sally said.

"I need March of last year."

As she walked to the bin containing the weekly issues from January, February, and March of 2016, Mark said, "What are we looking for, Detective Lang?"

After calling the students by first name, she was strangely upset that he was being formal with her.

"Steve, uh, Mr. Willis, said that there'd been an incident on campus involving Mr. Hamilton last spring. He said it was in the student paper and probably the local one, as well."

"The mugging. I remember that," Sally said, handing Courtney the issue dated March 15. The front page featured a band she'd never heard of that appeared at a recent campus fundraiser and a photo of a man with the caption, "Dean Andrews Denies Rumors of Teacher Strike."

"I'm sorry. I don't see the story," Courtney said scanning the page.

"Oh, it's not in the front." Sally took back the paper and flipped to an inside page that had a column labelled "Security Citings." Below several other campus incidents, was a brief mention of a "mugging of a male Sophomore near Stanley Hall."

At the word "mugging," Courtney flinched. Mark was looking over her shoulder as she read the article.

"Interesting. This was around the time of the Park Muggings, too. I wonder why they didn't connect them."

"All the others took place in the park, but the campus gates are only a mile from it." She turned to Sally. "Can we keep this?"

"Yeah. We have copies. Anything that can help."

"What do you remember about the mugging?" Mark asked.

"Joe was going to his economics class. He's, I mean he was, a business major." She choked a bit at the past tense. "Someone jumped him from behind near Stanley Hall, that's where the business classes are held. All the buildings on campus are named for people like the dorms. They took Joe's wallet, phone, and some cash. Not too much money. He worked part-time on campus in food services, but he never carried a lot on him. He didn't get much of a look at the guy, but he said he was wearing a mask."

"A mask?" That detail wasn't in the paper.

"Yeah. Like a black ski mask with holes for the eyes."

Courtney glanced at Mark and then back to Sally. "The Park Mugger wore a ski mask. Why weren't the police notified about this? Were there any witnesses?"

"No one saw anything. Joe was late that day, so most people were in classes. He didn't want to make a big deal out of it and refused to report it. He said he thought it was one of his friends playing a prank, but he never got the money or his phone back." She paused. "You don't think what happened to him then had anything to do with . . ."

That's exactly what Courtney thought, but how would she explain this to Sansone when the woman had ordered her not to reopen that old case?

"Right now, we're investigating all avenues," Mark replied to the girl's questions. "Thank you for showing us the paper."

Sally smiled up at him. "No problem, Detective." Was she flirting? Courtney was used to the way female witnesses acted around Mark, but why should she care since they were no longer involved?

"I'll walk you both back to Craig," Sally offered.

The guard locked up as they left the newsroom. Sally chatted with Mark as they went back downstairs. Courtney followed behind, feeling like a third wheel next to the campus cop.

When they got back to the dorm, police cars were still lined up outside.

"Thank you." Mark addressed Sally. "There are officers inside still working on this. They'll probably be around for a while, but I think we have what we need for now. We'll be in touch if we have any further questions." He included Courtney with a slight turn of his head.

"Do you need my number?" The girl seemed eager to give it to him.

"That's okay. We know how to reach you." Courtney was surprised he didn't add it to his cell contacts.

As Sally waved goodbye to them and rushed inside probably to return to Winchester, Mark asked if he could have the paper. Courtney handed it to him. "Are you going to show it to Sansone? Better you than me."

He quirked an eyebrow. "What does that mean?"

"I'm not on her good list right now."

"Oh?"

Courtney suddenly felt the night close in on her. It was late. She was tired, and she just wanted to go home and snuggle in bed with her cat.

"Nothing you need to know. Can you write this up? I'm really exhausted and want to get to bed." She ripped out a few pages from her pad and passed him the notes of her talk with Willis.

"Still using that antiquated method to record interviews?" He grinned.

She wasn't in the mood to be teased. "Goodnight, Mark." She turned and began walking to her car.

"Hey, wait up." He ran to catch her. Putting his arm on the hood as she opened the door, he said, "Before you leave, do you want to grab a quick drink with me? There's got to be a campus dive open somewhere or we can hit a nearby bar. I even have some good wine at my place."

"Mark, please. I said I was tired." She could use a drink, but not with him.

He took his hand off her car. "Okay. Rain check. We still need to talk."

She didn't reply but started the engine. He got the message and helped close her door. "Goodnight, Courtney. Sleep well."

# Chapter Five

Bill came into her office the next day. She was on her second cup of coffee and hadn't seen Mark since she got in.

"Good morning," he said without a smile. "I got wind of Sansone's argument with you yesterday. I also heard about the university murder."

She didn't bother looking up from the papers on her desk. Although she'd asked Mark to write up the report, she had jotted some notes from memory while they were still fresh in her mind. She had gone over them in a restless sleep the night before. The image of Joseph Hamilton staring at her through horrified eyes appeared in the few dreams she had.

"There was no argument, just a difference of opinion. Mark is handing in the report if you'd like to speak with him about it."

"Sansone will give it to me to look over. I agree with her, Courtney. Last year's muggings had nothing to do with the old lady's murder and even less with the college kid's. I'll put my money on the roommate's jealous girlfriend. Did you speak with her?"

"No. Mr. Willis was the only one I spoke with. He didn't mention a girlfriend, and I didn't ask. I doubt there was a triangle going on with his deaf friend. He had nothing but good things to say about the guy."

"When did you start believing everything a witness said? I think Sansone is right that you're slipping, Court."

She raised her head at that. "I don't appreciate your taking sides in this, Bill. Now please get out of my office if you don't have anything else to tell me."

He spun his chair around without a word and left. She felt as if she'd been punched. Gone were the days when Bill would joke with her about Sansone and back her up. Now her old partner was her adversary. It hurt.

Mark came in a few minutes later and tossed the report on her desk. "Check it out before I hand it in to Sansone. I want Bill to have a look, too."

"He's already been here. He and Sansone are buddies now."

Mark raised his eyebrows. She noticed he looked tired. He probably hadn't had much sleep last night either. "Sorry to hear that. I'm still your friend, though. You know that, right, Court?"

"I would think you would have difficulty staying friends with me under the circumstances."

"Not at all."

"Are you sure about that? Are you maybe hoping you can change my mind about us?"

"Not hoping. Praying." He walked back to the door. "Take your time looking at that. If you're afraid to drop it off with Sansone or Bill, you can just leave it for me. I should be back in an hour or so."

She pushed the papers aside. "Where are you going?" She wondered if he was following up on some leads he didn't want to share, but that was crazy. Even if they were no longer romantic partners, they were still work partners.

"I'm just heading to Evidence to take another look at what they got from McCarver's place. I wanted to compare it with the stuff from Hamilton's room."

"You're thinking the two cases might be connected?"

"I didn't say that. I just want to have a look. Want to join me?"

She hesitated. She never liked going downstairs to where they kept evidence from past and current crimes. The place gave her the creeps almost as badly as the forensic room across the hall from it where the bodies were examined before being transported to the morgue. She finally agreed to go because she had something else in mind. While she was there, she wanted to try to get her hands on the evidence from the Park Muggings. She had to prove to Sansone her theory that the perpetrator of the old crimes was responsible for the new ones.

\*\*\*

Bill was usually the one who spent time in Evidence since he was now restricted to the station and didn't go out in the field like she and Mark. That's why she wasn't surprised to see him when they entered the windowless room after signing in with Grace, the Evidence clerk.

"Thompson," Mark said as they joined him down the aisle where labelled file boxes contained items found at crime scenes.

He slid one of the boxes back into its slot. Courtney noticed it was luckily at eye level with him. He would have a problem reaching the higher ones, but she was sure Grace would assist him if he asked.

"My two favorite people," he said, turning his chair around to face them. She hated the sarcasm in his tone. "Don't worry. I'm on my way out. I'll leave you alone to your romantic rendezvous. Nice and private here most of the time except for us nosy cripples occasionally poking around."

Courtney was relieved that Mark didn't take the bait. All she needed was for him to punch Bill. Without a word, he simply stepped out of the way to let him pass. It could've been Courtney's overtired state or her imagination, but she could've sworn that Bill had placed something in the small bag attached to his wheelchair that he carried water or other items in that he couldn't fit in his pockets.

\*\*\*

When they were alone going through the slim contents of the evidence boxes, Mark said, "He's getting worse, Court. Do you know if he's still seeing his counselor?"

As part of his recovery process after the shooting, Bill had been seeing the department's psychologist, a woman named Myra who also acted as a crime profiler. She had not been of much help with the Park Muggings, and other than preventing Bill from committing suicide, she didn't seem to have done any good in correcting his attitude. Still, Courtney knew it was helpful to have someone to talk to. She regretted that she hadn't taken Mark's suggestion on speaking to Myra about her feelings over what happened to Bill and to her sister and mother.

"I have no idea, Mark. Maybe I should check with her."

Mark was gazing into the almost empty box that contained the evidence from Agnes' house. "You could, or you might want to talk to his brother."

After Bill had been released from the hospital, Rick had taken him in. Bill wasn't thrilled with the idea, even though he was close to his younger brother. He'd expected that his apartment could've been updated with ramps and bars and other accommodations for a disabled man, but Rick had insisted. Courtney believed it was his way of paying Bill back after bailing him out of some trouble with drugs he'd gotten into as a teenager. Since their parents were dead, Rick was the only relative who came to the hospital while Bill was there.

"I'll give Rick a call today," Courtney promised as Mark pushed the shoebox-sized container back into its slot. "Nothing here that can help us. You didn't want to look, did you?"

What Courtney wanted was to check the boxes next to the ones from Agnes' and Joe's crime scenes—the boxes that held the evidence for the Park Muggings. But would

Mark allow her to do that after he knew Sansone had made her agree to leave those cases alone?

"No. I trust that you didn't find anything of importance in McCarver's evidence box."

He shook his head. "Nada. The poor lady let her killer in. Since she was blind, she didn't see him coming and didn't have the strength to stop him once she knew what was happening. He choked her with his gloved hands. The only evidence at the scene belonged to her."

"What about the past incident? The one where her house was robbed. Was there evidence from that?"

Mark checked the labels of the boxes in the same row. Courtney's heart beat fast at the thought that the Park Muggings boxes were close to where he was looking. He pulled one out. "I think this is it. Want to have a look yourself?"

Courtney walked over. The space down the aisles was narrow. That was why they'd had to clear the area before Bill could maneuver his wheelchair out. As she stepped to where Mark was standing, she became aware of how close their bodies came. She thought of Bill's remark about a romantic rendezvous but pushed those words away from her mind. She caught a whiff of Mark's light cologne, a blend of woodsy spices, and couldn't help but feel a wave of attraction build in her stomach. She remembered being here with him once, how he'd pushed her against the cabinets, almost knocking down their contents, and kissed her madly. She could feel his tongue in her mouth probing, his hands strong and warm on her body. They'd almost made love, but Grace had called to them. Even so far away, she may have heard the noise and thought something had fallen. Mark had laughed as he told her all was okay back there. Now she wondered if, somehow, Bill had known what they'd been up to. He'd already come back to work by that time, so it was possible.

"Are you alright?" Mark asked, bringing her back to the present.

"Yes, I'm fine. What's in the box?" She took a deep breath as he pushed it toward her.

"Not much, I'm afraid. McCarver wasn't even home when the house was broken into. She was at dinner with her sister. When they got back, the door was ajar, and her jewelry case was empty. There wasn't anything of value among the stuff, mostly costume pieces, and the thief never found the money hidden under her mattress. I don't know why old people still hide cash in their houses."

Courtney was familiar with the case. She and Bill had worked on it. Mark was working in Evidence then. "Why did they bother keeping any evidence? She probably was reimbursed by insurance."

"Sansone's a stickler for details, remember? And this was around the time of the muggings."

Courtney didn't need to be told that. She looked inside the box and pulled out a small Ziploc that contained a black thread. "Was this identified?"

Mark was holding the paper that listed the contents of the box. "I think this is it. 'Black fiber possibly from a knit cap,'" he read.

Courtney suddenly remembered Agnes saying she didn't own any black hats. Also, the burglary took place in the summer. Who wears a knit cap in the heat? She suddenly felt faint in the enclosed space. *A thread from a ski mask could easily be mistaken for one from a knit hat,* she thought.

\*\*\*

Courtney never got the opportunity to check the Park Muggings evidence boxes, but it might've been just as well. When Mark noticed how pale she'd become after seeing the black fiber, he suggested they go back to the office, and she was relieved to take him up on it.

They spent the rest of the morning going over other cases. She didn't spend much time looking at the report Mark had written but had approved it for him to share with Sansone. Neither of them had discussed the episode in the Evidence room, but she felt he was following the same track as her when he said that he was sorry that Joe Hamilton hadn't reported his attack on campus because, at this late date, if any fibers from his assailant's mask had been found on campus, it would be too late to match them to the one found by Agnes McCarver's jewelry case.

"Were any fibers ever found at the mugging scenes?" she asked tentatively. She hoped, if he was beginning to see the similarities, that he could convince Sansone to reopen the investigation into those crimes.

"Possibly, but let's deal with McCarver's and Hamilton's cases first." Her hopes were dashed, and she knew he saw the disappointment on her face because he added, "Sorry, I know what you're thinking, Court, and I'm not ruling it out, but we have to start slow."

She sighed. "Last time, I was too slow, Mark, and Sansone still holds it against me. I don't want to make the same mistake. It cost Bill his legs."

"I was right. You still blame yourself for that."

"Yes, and so does Sansone it seems."

"Screw her."

"Shhh, Mark. She might be listening." Courtney put a finger against her lips to quiet him. Sansone was known for her stealthiness and for standing outside of offices with her ear to the doors.

"I don't care. She's got you afraid of your shadow, and I don't like that. You used to have a spine. I remember. When I first started here, you were my role model. I was so jealous of Bill having you as a partner. And, yes, I admit, as a girlfriend. But now I pity you more than I pity him. He and Sansone took away your nerve."

She had no reply to his accusations.

He stood up from his desk. "I need some fresh air. Want to go grab some lunch with me? It's after one already."

"It's twenty degrees outside, Mark. I'd rather stay here."

"Okay. I'll bring something back for you. Is Micky D's okay? I'm still on a budget."

"Just a salad, please."

As he left, she picked up the phone. She was going to take his advice to call Bill's brother. Rick was self-employed and worked from home, so she might be able to reach him while Bill was still at the station. He answered on the third ring. "Hello."

"Rick, it's Courtney. How are you?" She hoped her voice didn't betray her concern, but he knew there had to be a reason for her call.

"Courtney, hi. Is everything okay? Is Bill alright?"

"He's fine. He's here. I just wanted to chat with you about something. I'd rather he didn't know."

"Hmmm. Next week's his birthday. Is it about that?"

She'd completely forgotten. "No, but thanks for reminding me. We should do something for him. I'll get back to you on it. I actually called because…" she paused. How could she word it? "There's been some tension between Bill and Mark. It's gotten worse lately. He hasn't been so pleasant to me, either. Do you know if he's still seeing Dr. Klein?"

Rick sighed. "I'm afraid not, Courtney. I've noticed he's been more on edge lately. I hear him having nightmares at night."

"Maybe he should take some time off. I could speak with Sansone."

"No. Don't do that. He'd be worse at home. At least working gives him something to keep his mind off things."

"Not when he's constantly dealing with crimes. Can't he help you with your business?"

"I design websites. He's a cop. He wouldn't have the patience for it, and I wouldn't have the guts for police work. We both enjoy what we do. He's just going through a hard time right now."

"Do you have any idea why? I mean, he seemed to be adjusting up until a month ago."

"He may have just been acting. If you ask me, the bullet that crippled him also crippled his spirit. Your leaving him was the last straw, though. He still calls your name in his sleep."

She couldn't believe what she was hearing. "He told me to go, Rick."

"But you listened, and now you're with Mark."

"More of a reason for him to take off time, and I'm no longer with Mark, Rick."

"Oh? Sorry. Maybe the three of us should get together and talk. I can suggest you come to dinner one night. Would you?"

"Yes, but I'll bring the food. Why don't we do it next week for his birthday? I know he likes Italian. I'll try to speak to Dr. Klein before then and see if she has any suggestions for us."

"Sounds like a plan. Thanks for calling, Courtney."

"You're welcome, Rick." As she hung up the phone, Mark was back with lunch.

# Chapter Six

Myra Klein sat behind her desk looking at Courtney through the thick, square-shaped frames of her glasses that rode the bridge of her long nose. In the old days, or what Courtney referred to in her mind as BBC (before Bill was crippled), he used to call the staff psychologist Pinocchio behind her back. The thought brought a smile to Courtney's lips, but she wiped it off when she noticed the scrutinizing gaze of Klein's gray-blue eyes. She couldn't help but feel like a bug being observed under a microscope when she visited the woman. It wasn't her body that was under inspection, but her psyche, which was even worse.

"Hello, Courtney. It's been a while. I hope you've been well." She tucked a strand of coal black hair behind her ear where a tiny gold stud was nearly invisible against the lobe. "What can I do for you today?"

"Thanks for meeting with me, Dr. Klein. I'm fine. I'm not here about myself. I wanted to speak with you about a fellow officer."

"No problem, but please call me Myra. We've known each other long enough to be on a first-name basis."

Not only had they known one another since Courtney began working at the station ten years ago right out of the police academy, but they'd spent long hours discussing the Park Mugger's profile, and Klein had been a great support after Bill had been shot, assuring Courtney that she hadn't been responsible, even though the psychologist's words hadn't alleviated her guilt.

"Sure. I just feel odd calling you Myra. Sorry. It's an authority thing."

"But I'm not your superior." Klein took a gold-plated pen from the "Shrinks Have More Fun and Feel Less

Guilty About It" mug she used as a pen holder and placed it on an open notebook. Like Courtney, she preferred written notes to digital ones.

"I know. You remind me of my fifth-grade teacher, that's all."

The psychologist grinned. "What about your mother? I'm old enough."

She didn't want to go there. She'd never spoken to Klein about the fire even though she'd been invited to do so many times.

"No. If you don't mind, I have to get back to work soon. This is my lunch break. Sansone doesn't even know I made this appointment."

Klein raised her thin gray eyebrows. They didn't match the darkness of her hair which was obviously a dye job. "So, this isn't work related?"

"It is, but I'd rather she didn't know."

Klein began to jot something down on her pad. "Go on. Talk to me."

"It's about Bill."

"Ah." She looked back at Courtney with that disturbing intense gaze over her glasses. "I haven't seen him for several weeks. I've been wondering how he's doing."

"Not well." Courtney looked down into her lap where her hands were clasped. She felt a thumbnail cut into her palm and loosened them. "He's a different man, Myra, but you should know that. He seemed like he was adjusting when he first came back to the job, but now he's on a downward spiral. He's got a lot of anger issues with me and especially with Mark. I don't know how to handle him. I spoke with his brother, and I'm going to their house Wednesday night. It's his birthday. I offered to bring dinner, and I'll pick up a cake, too. But I don't know if he'll be happy about that. I asked Rick not to tell him. I have no idea what I'll say when I'm there. I thought maybe you could help."

Klein listened to Courtney's tale with the same penetrating gaze. She took a few minutes to reply, as Courtney tightened her fingers again. "Obviously, this means a lot to you. It seems that you haven't gotten over your feelings for Bill, and his anger is part of his unresolved feelings for you."

"He was the one who broke up with me." She really didn't want to rehash all of this, but that's what psychologists did—they made you face things you wanted kept hidden from yourself.

"Let me ask you this, Courtney. Do you really think Bill would've expected you to stay with him, take care of him, and act as his nurse?"

Before she could reply, Myra continued as if she hadn't even asked her a question. "You have to understand that men are very sensitive and proud. He equated the loss of his legs with the loss of his manhood."

"But there are plenty of disabled people who live normal lives, marry, even have children," Courtney pointed out.

"Yes, but there are many others, like Bill, who shut themselves off from the ones they love. He's frustrated and hurt. When I counseled him, he told me some things …" She put down her pen.

Courtney's stomach lurched. "What things?" She'd never told Klein about Bill's proposal. Had he?

Klein rested her hands back on her pad. "We went over that night several times. I can't reveal what is told to me in confidence, but I will say that he needs you back in his life. Not as a lover, perhaps, but as a friend. It's going to take time. He may never come to terms with Mark, who he sees as the man he once was, his replacement, if you will."

"I'm through with Mark," she put in before the psychologist could finish.

"Doesn't matter. It won't change the way he feels, and you shouldn't put your life on hold because of it. I know you need to return to work but let me ask you one last thing before you go. If Bill had asked you to marry him before he was shot, would you have said, yes?"

Courtney sat there stunned. She looked down at her hands. Her nail had cut into the skin, and there was blood across her palm.

***

She had to take a break. She still had some time left to her lunch hour, and she could extend it if she wanted. It was warmer than normal for the end of January, and the sunny chill helped clear her mind. As she walked to her car in the staff parking lot, she breathed in deeply. The interview with Myra had cost her. She should've been more prepared for the psychologist's probing questions.

She found herself driving toward Edna Black's house. She had meant to pay her a visit earlier in the week and see how Chirpy was doing, too.

Edna opened the door after checking the peephole and unlatching several locks. She imagined they'd been added since her sister's death. "Hello. Detective Lang, is it?"

"Yes, but please call me Courtney." She recognized the small room into which she was led. It had similar furnishings to Agnes' but brighter patterns and paint. The apricot walls added a nice contrast to the dark brown sofa and wingback chair. Chirpy's cage stood in the corner. The bird was sitting on his perch. When she approached, he said, "Visitor. Nice lady."

"Thank you, Chirpy. I see you've made yourself at home here."

Edna smiled. "Have a seat, Courtney. Can I bring you anything—tea or a sandwich? I was about to make myself lunch."

Courtney didn't want to put the woman to any trouble, but she found herself still hungry after the quick lunch at the station with Mark. "If you don't mind, a cup of tea and a sandwich would be lovely."

Courtney took the chair by the bird cage as Edna went to the kitchen to prepare the food. She returned a few minutes later with a teapot on a tray and two peanut butter and jelly sandwiches spread with just the right amount of jelly and peanut butter.

"I hope you like herbal tea. It's peppermint, soothing for the stomach; and, of course the sandwich. My husband always liked PB&J's, and so did Agnes. We ate them a lot as children. Our mother packed it for our school lunches. In those days, they weren't worried about allergies, and less kids had them, too. It's the environment, you ask me. All these cell phone stations and automobiles with their gas emissions."

Courtney nodded as she took another bite of the sandwich and washed it down with the tea after she'd blown on the cup to cool the liquid.

"I'm glad you came by," Edna continued. "It's just been me and Chirpy. A few of my friends came to visit after they heard the news, but then they went back to their own lives. I can't expect people to make time for an old woman. I miss Aggie so much." Her pale blue eyes, so like her sister's, started to water as if she was about to cry. Courtney decided to change the subject.

"Are there any senior groups that you could join? Do you go to church, or maybe the library offers some programs you'd be interested in? I could check for you if you'd like."

She shook her head as she took a bite of her sandwich. She was seated next to Courtney, her hands shaking a little as she picked up her tea cup. "That's very sweet of you, but I'll be fine. I'm not that social a person. Aggie was. Even with her disability, she managed to make friends easily. Of course, as the years passed, she kept more to herself in that house. I wish she would've taken me up on my offer for her to live here. It would've been good for both of us, and maybe..." she paused. "What's the use? You can't cry over spilt milk. You can't take back time, can you?"

The woman was wise. Did she have any idea how much the words she spoke meant to Courtney?

***

Courtney left Edna's house a short time later. Before she'd gone, she'd asked about Agnes' robbery last May, two weeks before the Park Muggings began. Edna recounted how she and Agnes had attended a play, one of their rare outings that was a birthday treat to Agnes from her sister. When Edna had dropped Agnes home, she noticed the door was ajar. Agnes ran in, fearing for Chirpy's safety, but found her parrot unharmed in his cage. Edna helped her sister check the rest of the house, and they discovered her jewelry armoire hanging open, a pile of rings, bracelets, and assorted trinkets scattered on her bedroom rug.

"We called the police immediately. You came with a handsome cop you said was your partner. Do you remember?"

"I do," Courtney replied. "You both were pretty frazzled."

"It was upsetting, but you and your good-looking partner were so kind and helped us calm down. Is he still working with you? There was another man who came with you to talk to me after Aggie's death." She choked on the last word.

"He's my new partner," Courtney explained. "Detective Thompson still works at the station, but he had an, uh, accident last summer."

"Oh, my gosh. So sorry to hear that. I hope it wasn't anything serious."

Courtney refrained from going into detail about Bill's shooting. "He's coming along. I need to leave soon, but is there anything you remember that's similar from what you saw at your sister's house when you found her to the burglary that occurred last spring?"

Edna paused. "Do you think the same person who robbed Aggie also killed her?"

"It's a possibility. She wasn't home when her jewelry was stolen. We're considering that the burglar came back to steal more valuables and she tried to stop him."

"I don't think my sister would've done that. She would've let him take everything. She didn't have expensive possessions. Her most treasured item was Chirpy."

"In any case, we have to consider all angles. Do you remember anything at all that might connect the two crimes?" Courtney hated pushing the old woman for information, but the black fiber in the evidence box that she'd uncovered couldn't be ignored.

"I'm sorry, Detective. My memory is not as good as it used to be. When I found Aggie, I didn't pay attention to anything except the fact she wasn't breathing. I'm the older sister. She should've gone to my funeral and not me to hers." Tears sprang to her eyes as she said those words.

Courtney reached out and squeezed the woman's bony hand. "I'm so sorry, Edna. Forgive me for my persistence, but it's part of the investigation."

"I know. You're only doing your job, my dear. It's okay. I've got Chirpy now, and he helps cheer me up. I must be strong for him. It's what Agnes would want."

As if understanding his new owner's words, the bird said, "Love you."

Edna smiled through her drying tears. "See? What did I tell you?"

# Chapter Seven

She was in the park at night walking on a trail of twigs and pinecones. There was some litter, too— napkins that flew off a picnic table, pop-tops from scrunched-up beer cans, mounds of Canada Geese droppings from the nearby lake. She avoided these by stepping around them. A light, warm wind rustled her hair and the lapels of her uniform. A scent of evergreens and pine filled her nostrils. And then—a scream pierced the night. She ran in the direction of the sound, her heart beating, a chill taking the place of the summer heat. She fingered her gun, ready to draw it, scanning the area around her as she ran.

"Courtney. Over here. Help me." She stopped abruptly upon hearing her name. She recognized the voice. It was Bill. He lay on the ground bleeding from a wound in his back. She tore off her police vest, bent down, and tried to staunch the blood, but it kept spreading into the grass, onto her hands.

"What happened, Bill? Who did this?"

"Leave me, Court. Go get him. He has her." He pointed weakly toward a copse of trees.

She dropped her gun and searched for her phone to call for backup, but she couldn't find it.

"I can't leave you." Tears gathered in her eyes. She went to wipe them and felt the wet blood glide across her face.

"Go, Courtney. Don't worry about me. It's the Park Mugger. Catch him. He's taken her hostage."

Against her better judgement, she picked up her gun and ran toward the trees Bill had indicated. Then she saw them—a masked man holding Myra with a knife against her throat.

"Let her go," she demanded, "or I'll shoot."

The masked man ignored her. "I'm not afraid of you or your lover," he said. "I know he asked you to marry him."

"What is that to you, and what about her? She's innocent."

"She knows too much. She knows you never would've accepted his proposal because I'm the one you love." He moved the knife closer to Myra's throat and a thin cut dripped blood. Myra's eyes bulged through her eyeglass lenses.

Courtney felt her finger pull back the trigger. She aimed for his eyes and squeezed. The bullet hit him in the center of his ski mask. He collapsed, releasing his victim and dropping the knife to the ground.

Courtney ran to Myra. "Are you okay?"

"Yes, I'm fine thanks to you, but Bill was shot. You should get back to him."

"I will, but I need to know who shot him." She bent down to remove the bloody ski mask from the Park Mugger's face. When it was off, she stared down into Mark's dead eyes and screamed.

She woke with the blankets on the floor and a cold sweat covering her body. She was so jumpy from the dream that she almost had a heart attack when Oliver jumped up next to her and started demanding his breakfast with loud meows. As she got up to feed him, she checked the alarm by her bed. It was 10 a.m. Oh, God, she was late for work. How did she sleep so long? It felt as if she'd just nodded off and had the nightmare.

As soon as she'd fed Oliver a can of his favorite Friskies seafood pate and poured some kibble and water into his other dishes, she heard someone knocking on her door. She was still in her nightclothes so went back into her bedroom and donned a robe. Remembering the dream, she also grabbed her gun. Mark stood on her doorstep with two cups of coffee and a bag of bagels from the local deli. "Hey, don't shoot the messenger. I'm just bringing you breakfast."

"Sorry. I had a bad night."

"You look it. I figured you overslept. You probably needed to. I told Sansone you weren't feeling well but that I would check on you. Can I come in, or would you rather I leave this?"

She waved him inside. "That was nice of you. I had a crazy dream. A nightmare. I'm still on edge from it. I need some time to come to terms with it. The breakfast will help. Thank you."

He set the coffee cups and bag on the kitchen table, got some plates and napkins and laid everything out. "It's been a while since we sat down to breakfast together. I picked up some everything bagels and the scallions and chives spread you like. Want to tell me about the dream?"

The bagels were pre-cut. She rolled the spread on one half, bit into it, and then sipped some coffee. The warm liquid helped dispel the chills that still quaked through her body. "I'd rather not, Mark."

"No problem." He spread his own bagel and gulped down his coffee. "I know you need time to get ready, but don't rush. When I finish eating, I can go back and tell Sansone you'll be in as soon as you're up to it—or you can take the day off." His blue eyes surveyed her. She could tell he was concerned.

"No. I'm fine. It was just a dream. I won't be long. If you can wait for me, we can go back together."

He nodded. "I don't mind waiting."

As they ate in silence, Oliver brushed against Mark's ankles and purred. He bent down and pet him. When they were seeing one another, the cat had grown fond of him. Although he didn't have any pets of his own, Mark was great with animals. He told Courtney that he had a bunch of them when he was young and if he hadn't gone into policework, he might've wanted to be a vet.

The coffee began to clear her head, although fragments of the dream still lingered. The subconscious plays weird tricks—Mark, a thief and killer, Myra, a victim? She pushed the memory of the dream away.

"I saw Edna yesterday and Chirpy."

"Oh? How are they doing?" Mark didn't seem upset that she had visited them without him.

"As well as possible, I guess. Chirpy's settling in well. Edna misses her sister, but that's to be expected. She's by herself now, but at least she has the bird for company."

Mark finished his coffee. "Was it just a social visit, or did you question her about the murder?"

She looked down and gave him the answer. "I didn't want to push her, but I asked about the burglary last May. She didn't remember anything."

"You're going on the theory that the same person committed both?"

She raised her eyes to his. "Yes, and that Agnes' killer was also the Park Mugger."

"Whoa. That's a stretch."

"Mark, don't you see? The muggings started just two weeks after Agnes' house was burglarized. She lives only a few blocks from the park."

"I understand, but Sansone is not going to buy it. What about Joe Hamilton? The college is not far from the park either, but he was mugged on campus two months earlier."

"It still fits."

"Okay. I'll tell you what. I was planning on going back to the college today and talking to Joe's roommate and Winchester Palmer. Would you like to go with me?"

She felt unreasonably happy that he had invited her when he knew she'd done some investigating without him.

"Sure. Mark, there's one other thing." She wanted to tell him about her talk with Myra and the upcoming dinner with Bill and his brother.

He glanced at his watch. "We don't have much time. I have to check in back at the station and hand in a few reports before we can go to the campus."

"It's okay then. We can talk on the ride back." She excused herself to shower and dress while Mark cleared the table and waited for her in the living room. As the warm water soothed her body that was still slightly chilled, she decided not to tell Mark anything else. She hated keeping things from him because he usually had a way of finding out; but where Bill was concerned, it would only strain their relationship. Although she had no intention of resuming their romance, she hoped they could remain friends as well as co-workers.

"What else did you want to tell me?" Mark asked as they were driving to work. He'd offered to take her in his car, and she'd agreed. She still felt shaky and wouldn't be comfortable behind the wheel yet.

"Nothing." She hated lying, but she'd decided it was best not to share her discussion with the psychologist. "I was just curious as to what you were thinking of questioning Willis and Palmer about."

"The same. It's always good to repeat questions. People sometimes remember things when asked again."

"Or they have time to fashion some lies."

He grinned. "That's true. In either case, we might learn something new."

She changed the subject. "It's colder today."

"Yes. The wind chill is kicking in." He adjusted the car's heater. She was glad he hadn't brought along the squad car. The heater took forever to come up in the one they used.

"Do you think it's going to snow?"

"Feels like it. Smells like it, too." He'd rolled up his window that he'd kept slightly ajar when he'd put on the heat.

"What kind of mood is Sansone in today?" Another topic change. Anything to keep their conversation impersonal.

"Not any better than yesterday. There were flowers delivered for her. They were from Bill."

"You're kidding." She was surprised and disappointed the topic had turned to her previous partner.

"I think he's kissing up to her. It's part of his campaign to make me look bad." The earlier lightness in his voice had tightened.

"Don't be paranoid, Mark."

"I can't help it, Court. I don't care that he's disabled. I don't care that he's probably still in love with you. The guy's got it out for me, and I can't do anything about it because we work together. You don't know how frustrating it is to be in this situation."

"I can imagine." She did. It frustrated her just as badly that the two men she admired most were at each other's throats.

"It's okay. I'm trying to deal with it." He pulled into the police station's employee parking lot. "I'm thinking of talking with Klein. Do you think she'd help?"

Now was her chance to tell him about her own discussion with the psychologist, but she hesitated. Myra wouldn't reveal that they'd spoken. "You could give it a shot, Mark. I don't think it would hurt."

He parked the car. "That's what I'm thinking. Okay, we're here. Let's check in with Sansone, I'll hand in my reports, and then we'll head to the college."

\*\*\*

Despite the twenty-degree weather, Courtney couldn't help but notice the unseasonal way students were dressed as she and Mark walked through campus to Stanley Hall. She was bundled up in her cocoa coat wearing brown leather gloves, a hat, and winter boots. Mark wore similar clothes minus the boots; and instead of a coat, he had a padded vest over his uniform.

"Those kids are going to freeze," she commented as three giggling coeds rushed into the dorm wearing only short-sleeved sweaters and jeans.

Mark grinned. "The cold doesn't bother young people, especially not girls. They like to show off their bodies without constraints. I'm sure you dressed that way when you were their age, Court. You probably don't remember."

She shrugged. "It's not that long ago, Mark, but you're right."

As they entered the building, Mark explained that he had called Winchester on his cell and arranged for him and Steve to meet them during a free period. It wasn't difficult to set a time because both men started classes later in the day on Mondays.

The two of them were at the desk when Courtney and Mark arrived. Winchester shook their hands, but Steve stood back, a short shadow behind the taller Resident Assistant.

"Thanks for meeting with us," Mark told them. "Is there somewhere we can talk that's private?"

"We have a lounge upstairs. It's not usually occupied at this hour," Winston replied.

They followed him up the stairs, behind more giggling women in summer clothing. Willis fell back behind them. Something made Courtney curious about the relationship between the two students. They didn't seem to be friends. Also, Winchester's girlfriend wasn't in sight. It was possible she was in class.

The room into which they were led featured a sofa, large-screen TV, two computers, a pool table, and a tall cabinet.

"Nice digs," Mark said. She thought he was trying to sound cool to impress the co-eds. "What's in there?" He pointed to the cabinet.

"We keep board games in there. Believe it not, we like to play those once in a while," Winchester said.

Courtney noticed the lock on the cabinet. "Why keep it locked? Do people steal the game pieces?"

Winchester smiled. "No, but sometimes guys store beer in there. Not all of us are drinking age."

"I remember those days," Mark said, still trying to bond with the younger men.

"I thought you were in charge of enforcing the rules around here," Courtney pointed out. She noticed Steve was standing quiet in the corner.

"Well, you know, I like to have fun, too. Have a seat, Detectives. Take off your coats." He glanced to include both of them.

Mark sat on the end of the sofa after removing his vest, and Courtney sat next to him. Winchester sat next to her, but Steve remained standing.

"Hey, man, what's wrong? There's plenty of room for you on the couch." He moved closer to Courtney, and she smelled his aftershave. She had kept her coat on even though heat was blasting through the room. *No wonder college tuition is so high if they waste money with overheating the buildings,* she thought.

Steve shrugged. "I'd rather stand. This isn't going to take long, is it? I have a chem exam in a half hour. I really should be studying."

"Don't worry. This won't take much time," Mark assured him. "We already wrote our report about what you've both told us regarding Mr. Hamilton's murder, but we realize that you were shocked and upset that night, so we wanted to ask again if either of you have remembered anything else that happened before or after Hamilton was found in the room? We also want to know if you have anything to add about his previous mugging?"

Winchester glanced at Steve. Courtney had the feeling that something passed between them, a code of some sort they shared with their eyes. Then Winchester looked back toward her and Mark. "Nope. Sorry to waste your time, but I have nothing new to add."

"What about you, Mr. Willis?" Mark probed looking toward Steve. Courtney thought he'd been aware of the same silent exchange between the two men.

"Me neither. Sorry," Steve said, but his eyes were focused down on the dirty square tiles of the rec room.

*\*\**

When they were outside, a few snowflakes were falling. "They were hiding something," Courtney said.

"I know." Mark had his hands in his pockets. He hadn't bothered to wear gloves.

"Should we try to talk to Steve alone another time?"

"Maybe. While we're still on campus, we can talk to someone at Security and the Dean. One of them might know something else, if not about the murder night, then at least about the previous crime. Even though Hamilton didn't report it, there was the mention in the campus crime blotter."

"That makes sense, but I don't think we can question these people without an appointment."

"We can, but we already have one." He glanced at his watch as a few fat flakes covered its face. He wiped them away with a bare hand and glanced up at the gray sky. "Looks like the snow is getting heavier, and it's almost time for us to see the Dean. It's not that far a walk." He indicated a hill that rose to their left. "Mind walking?"

"No. At least I'm dressed for the weather." She was glad to breathe in the refreshing snow-filled air after the stifling heat of the dorm.

\*\*\*

Dean Claire Clark appeared to be in her late forties, younger than Courtney pictured her. When Courtney attended school at Baxter, Dean Warren was in office. He was in his seventies.

"Thank you for seeing us," Mark said as he took one of the wooden chairs by the door that the Dean indicated. Courtney sat in the other. She felt like a student facing the principal for misbehaving.

"No problem at all," the Dean said, looking at them with small gray eyes. "I understand this is about Mr. Hamilton's unfortunate incident."

Courtney knew she'd used that term instead of murder because anything that happened on campus reflected on the administration.

"Yes, it does," Mark said. "What happened a few days ago and last year."

Clark raised her reddish eyebrows. They matched her hair shade so well that Courtney knew both came from the same bottle. "I'm afraid I'm not familiar with any incident from last year."

Mark reached into his vest pocket and withdrew the newspaper page about Joe's mugging. He placed it in front of her on the desk.

She looked down at it. "No name is listed here. I had no idea."

"Who submits the campus crime reports to the paper?"

"The head of Security."

"And who would that be?"

"Burt Connors, but Jose Sanchez was here at that time. He's no longer employed by us."

Courtney saw the light behind Mark's eyes that signaled his interest. "Do you know where he is now?"

She shook her head. "I don't keep track of my previous employees."

"Did he leave, or was he let go?" Courtney asked.

"He left. I think he found a position elsewhere. He gave us very little notice, but he hadn't been working with us long, and these things happen..." She waved her hands in a gesture of dismissal and Courtney noticed a gold band on her wedding finger. The dean was a Mrs.

"When did he go?" Mark asked.

"I don't really keep track of facts like that. I could check with my secretary."

"Can you just give us an estimate? Was it recent?"

She shook her head. "I have a meeting in a few minutes. I'm sorry, but I can't spend much more time answering questions."

Courtney saw the woman appeared flustered. She hadn't mentioned an upcoming meeting when they'd arrived.

Mark got up, dropped his card on the desk as he took back the newspaper. Then he signaled to Courtney to follow him. As they turned toward the door, the dean called to them. "It was nice meeting both of you. If I recall anything, I'll give you a call, Detective Farrell."

"Thank you," Mark said. As he placed his hand on the doorknob to pull it open, Clark added, "Mr. Sanchez left us last March. I believe it was shortly after the date of that newspaper report."

# Chapter Eight

When Courtney arrived home, there was a blinking light on her answering machine. One message. She considered it might be an advertiser but played it anyway. It was her aunt Violet asking her to call back. She hadn't spoken to Violet in over a month and was worried something was wrong with her or Uncle Vince. She dialed the phone with shaky fingers. She was still upset from the interviews at the college. Mark had promised her he'd locate Sanchez, and they might be able to find out what he knew about Hamilton's mugging and if that was the reason he left his job.

Violet answered on the second ring. She sounded calm and serene, as she always did. The woman would be unshaken in the middle of a hurricane. Courtney envied her sense of peace. It was due to that that Courtney had survived her mother's and sister's funeral.

"Hello, Courtney, dear. You haven't called or even emailed your old aunt in so long. I was just checking to see how you were doing."

"I'm fine," she lied. "Are you and Uncle Vince well?"

"We're wonderful. I make sure he takes his blood pressure pills, and we go for walks every day. You really should visit us down here again. It's lovely. You can get out of cold Connecticut."

"I can't, Aunt Violet. I'm in the middle of a case."

"I understand, but all work and no play isn't healthy. Talking about play, how is Bill doing? I feel so bad for that handsome man of yours, but I'm sure you're taking good care of him."

Courtney had not yet told her aunt that she and Bill had broken up after the shooting. For some reason, she was embarrassed to let her know. Now, she thought she should say something before her aunt found out herself. "Actually, we're not together anymore. He broke it off."

"Oh, no. Sorry to hear that, dear. I know it's hard for men to deal with a disability. Did you assure him it didn't make a difference to you?"

Courtney had tried to do that, but Bill refused to listen. "I tried, Aunt Violet. He's stubborn. He insisted."

Her aunt paused, and she could almost hear the waves near her Florida home. "I think you should keep trying, dear, if he means that much to you. There are so many services for the disabled today. He can live a regular life. He's still working—which means a lot—isn't he?"

"Yes, but he's restricted to a desk job."

"That's okay. He still gets up every morning and goes to work. That's important." Violet paused and then her voice, still calm, rose an octave. "Is it the sex that's the problem? You told me he was still functioning down there. You know there are plenty of positions that you could try."

"Aunt Violet, please. It's not the sex. I mean we haven't had any, but . . ."

"Well, that's it, then. He's frustrated. You need to show him he's still attractive to you. There must be some websites that can help. I'll Google them and email you the links."

"Stop!" Courtney didn't mean to raise her voice, but this conversation was getting way out of hand. "I have a new partner now. We started to date. I broke it off with him recently. I'm taking a break from relationships now."

"I can't tell you what to do, Courtney, but I can give you some advice. I dated a few men before I married your uncle, but I knew what was in my heart. If Vince had become disabled, it wouldn't have mattered to me. I wouldn't have turned my back on him and found someone else. I would've been faithful even if he turned me away. I would've remained loyal and shown him I still loved him."

Now Courtney was angry, but the tears that filled her eyes were those of guilt. She tried to keep her words from choking. "I have to go now, Aunt Violet."

"Alright. Keep that in mind and give my regards to Bill. Look for my email. I'll be sending you those links."

Courtney said goodbye and hung up. Her whole body was shaking as she fought back tears. Oliver came to rub against her legs, and she was thankful for the distraction. He wanted his dinner. It would give her something to do instead of pondering her aunt's advice.

***

Courtney wasn't surprised that she had another dream that night when she finally fell asleep. This one wasn't a nightmare. She was with Bill, running through the sand on a beach. They had spent several weekends at the beach last June before the fatal night he was shot.

She was laughing as he pursued her toward the water. She wore her blue bikini and slipped off her sandals by the water's edge as she entered the ocean. Bill was right behind her. He grabbed her around the waist. She turned in his arms, and he kissed her. They swam together, neatly matching each other's swim strokes. It was as if they were two fish with one body. Happiness bubbled up with her mixing with the frothy waves. Sailboats bobbed in the distance; sea gulls swooped toward shore. It was a perfect day.

She woke with the scene still in her mind. Had Aunt Violet been right? Had she given up on Bill too easily?

***

The next day at work, Mark greeted her with a cup of coffee and a smile on his face. "I found him."

At first, she was too disoriented to know who he was referring to, but then she remembered he'd been looking for the security guard who had worked on campus when Joe Hamilton was mugged.

She took the cup and walked with him into the office. "That's great. Have you arranged an interview?"

"Yep." He went to his desk and took some papers off it. "You should look at this first, though. He hid it from the college because the records were sealed, but I managed to have them opened."

Courtney glanced down at the report on Sanchez. It seemed he had a record. At sixteen, he'd been placed into juvie for several B&E's and one drugstore robbery.

"Interesting. Do you think he's our suspect?"

"Could be, but I have no idea how he'd be connected to McCarver. We need to talk to him. He seemed compliant enough when I called. It looks like he's been clean after his teen years."

"When's the appointment?" Courtney placed the papers back on the desk.

"Now. I was just waiting for you." He grabbed his own coffee. "If you're ready, let's go."

As they passed Bill's office, Courtney couldn't help but notice him sitting as his desk, head down, the same despondent look on his face. She remembered that tomorrow was his birthday and that she was bringing dinner and a cake for him and his brother. Maybe she could at least salvage their friendship.

*** 

Jose Sanchez was a short man, with big brown eyes shaded by long lashes, and a very thin gray moustache that matched his curly gray hair. He had a few cracked teeth and some scars from what had probably been an acne-ridden adolescence. Despite the season, he wore a sleeveless shirt which displayed a large dragon tattoo on his arm. Courtney thought it looked like a gang mark.

When Mark knocked on the ex-campus security guard's door and identified them as the police, Sanchez answered with a wary expression. "I know what you want." As he let them in, he added, "It's about Joe Hamilton. Am I right?" The words came out with a Latino accent.

Courtney knew he'd had time to think about their visit after Mark had called him, but she hadn't expected him to be so forthright.

"How did you guess?" Mark asked.

"I heard about his murda. Awful ding. Come. Sit. I live alone. Want some beer? Smokes?"

Mark declined both but took a seat on the tattered couch. Courtney sat next to him.

"Neither of you want anything?"

"No, thank you," Courtney said.

Sanchez grabbed a beer for himself from the small cooler in the living room. She wondered if he used it just for drinks. He sat across from them on a box crate. Courtney noticed the room seemed bare of photos but contained plenty of religious paintings and a cross over the door. The man lived like a bachelor, and he'd already explained that he was single; whether divorced, widowed, or never married was yet to be seen. It was likely in his file, but she hadn't looked too closely.

Sanchez took a cigarette out of the pocket of his trousers along with a lighter and lit it. Alternately, he smoked a few puffs, and then drank from the beer can in his other hand. Obviously, he wasn't health conscious, and Courtney was sensitive to the smoke. It burned her throat and caused her to start coughing. It also brought back memories she wanted to forget.

"You can step outside if you'd feel more comfortable, Detective Lang," Mark said, noticing her discomfort.

"No, please." Sanchez stubbed the cigarette out in a nearby ashtray lined with butts. "I know some people get sick from smoke. I've been puffin' since I was fourteen. Haven't gotten cancer yet and don't have the willpower to quit." Courtney thought of his juvenile record. So did Mark. He said, "We did a background check on you and found it a bit odd that the university hired you to head security when you had a record."

Sanchez took a sip of beer and swigged it around his mouth like mouthwash. "That was a long time ago. A buddy of mine got me in trouble. I've been clean since then. I found God. I go to mass every Sunday. I confess my sins."

Mark looked like he doubted the man's words, but he continued his questions. "You were working at Baxter when Mr. Hamilton's wallet was stolen on campus?"

"That's right."

"You sent the information to the campus newspaper, but you didn't call the police."

"Joe told me not to do that."

"But he allowed you to print the crime in the paper."

Sanchez lowered his eyes. "Not exactly, but I thought it might help other kids be more cautious. I didn't want to see someone else get robbed."

"But there weren't any other robberies since then, although two weeks later, the Park Muggings began."

"I heard of those. What of it?" He raised his eyes back toward Mark.

"One of the reporters on the campus paper told us the man who robbed Hamilton was wearing a mask. Did he hear it from you? It wasn't in the paper."

Sanchez gulped down another swallow of beer. "Maybe. I don't know."

"You left shortly after that. Why?"

Sanchez suddenly looked toward Courtney. "Doesn't she have any questions for me? Why you doing all the talking?"

Courtney still felt the soreness of the smoke in her throat. It reminded her of that terrible day ten years ago. "I'm just accompanying my partner. Answer his question." Her words came out a bit hoarse.

Sanchez finished his beer, paused, and then said, "I think I want my lawyer."

"You're not a suspect . . . yet," Mark told him.

"I prefer not to answer any more questions unless the lady wants to speak with me privately." He gave Courtney a leer that made her shudder.

"I don't think so. Let's get out of here, Detective Lang." Mark rose from the couch.

When they were outside, Courtney took large gulps of the cold air to clear her throat. "Why didn't you let me question him alone?"

"You saw the way he was looking at you."

"You could've waited outside. I am carrying a gun."

"He was bluffing. Believe me. Whatever he knows, he's keeping to himself."

They were back in the patrol car. Instead of putting on the heat, Mark rolled down the windows knowing that Courtney was still trying to rid her lungs of the tobacco. "Besides, being in that atmosphere wasn't doing you any good. The whole place reeked of smoke."

Mark knew Courtney's background. They'd been friends since he'd joined the department, but he'd never made a move on her because she was with Bill. When they'd started seeing one another after she and Bill broke up and she was assigned as his partner, Courtney told him about her family over too many glasses of wine one night. That was the same night they'd made love for the first time.

"Do you think he's guilty?"

"No, but I still don't like the guy. I hate religious hypocrites." Courtney had not yet met Mark's family, but he often spoke of his strict religious upbringing by a single mother who was now remarried. As a grown man, Mark had rebelled against the church and Margaret Farrell, his mother, who had been a coke addict.

\*\*\*

It turned out that Mark's instincts about Sanchez were right. When they returned to the station, the place was in an uproar.

"What's going on?" Courtney asked as she observed officers whispering together, and the looks people turned on them as they entered. Bill came down the hall and stopped when he saw them. There was a slight smile on his face as he greeted them. "Sansone's been looking for you two. There's been another one. The Handicapped Strangler has struck again."

# Chapter Nine

Gloria Fredericks was amazing. At thirty-two, she was an accomplished concert pianist for the Philharmonic. But it had taken years of practice, refusing social invitations, ignoring men that might've made good husbands, concentrating solely on her career. Her parents were proud and never seemed to worry about what their daughter had given up. Unlike the mothers of her unmarried friends, Francine Fredericks couldn't care less about becoming a grandmother. In fact, she worried it would make her appear old. A former model, she regretted having had to abandon her career after becoming pregnant with Gloria at twenty-one and marrying a stodgy but rich pianist who left his wife for her.

Moving to Baxter had afforded Gloria the escape from her bickering parents and their million-dollar home on the North Shore of Long Island where every room featured a piano. They had objected, of course. They had pleaded with her to stay with them. She'd compromised by promising to visit on weekends and continue her lessons with the teacher who would travel to Connecticut three times a week in a town car they agreed to hire for that purpose.

Although she hadn't broken completely free of her gilded cage, she was free to fly from it in the small Connecticut town. She hadn't made many friends the first few months in Baxter, but a terrible accident showed her that there were things more important than money. Driving home from her parents one Sunday night, tired from the grueling practice session they'd put her through, she crashed her car. Her airbags failed to deploy, and her right arm went through the window. After hours of surgery, she woke up to her mother screaming at the doctor because her daughter's arm couldn't be salvaged. It had been amputated.

Even though her parents begged her to move back with them and her mother threatened to sue the doctor who had performed her amputation, Gloria chose to stay in her small house in Connecticut. She managed to take care of herself, retraining her left arm to be the one she used for everyday tasks. Her piano sat idle. She never so much as touched the keys with her one hand. She avoided even listening to music. She felt she was coping the best she could, stopped calling her parents, and tried to make a life for herself. And then, after she'd accepted her limitations, someone broke in while she was shopping and stole one of the few expensive items she'd taken from home—her favorite painting of two young girls playing the piano that sat over her Wurlitzer. She'd filed a report with the police, but the Renoir was never recovered. Her father found out about it and made sure the insurance reimbursed her, but she kept the spot over the piano bare.

After the robbery, Gloria became even more of a hermit. She started having her groceries delivered by Peapod, a popular food delivery service. One day, she noticed the delivery man was not Greg, the one who normally brought her packages, and he wasn't driving the usual Peapod truck. But when he knocked on the door, he called, "Ms. Fredericks. Peapod. My truck broke down, but I wanted to make sure you got your groceries on time, so I'm using my own car."

She figured Greg was out sick or doing another route, and the guy at the door looked somewhat familiar. She'd seen him around Baxter, but she couldn't place where. Most likely, it had been at the grocery store. But when she let him in, she didn't expect him to grab her by her good arm and pin it behind her back. She flailed at him with her prosthesis, but couldn't reach him, so she tried to kick him. But he was strong and determined. As he dragged her into the bedroom with her stumbling against him, she begged him to let her go. He dropped her, and she fell on her hands and knees, gasping.

Before she could react, there was a cord around her throat, cinching it closed. Her eyes grew blurry as he tightened it. "Useless arm," she heard him say as he gazed down at her prosthesis. "You have a reason to die." As she realized the life was ebbing out of her, she heard a sound in the distance. Musical notes rose over his evil words. A piano was playing. She saw herself seated in front of it, fingers of both hands flying over the keys. As she struck a chord, she took her last breath.

***

Sansone sat at her desk, her face sharper than an iceberg. She looked at them over her long nose. "I can just see the headlines. 'Amputee murdered by Handicapped Strangler.'" We're stuck between a rock and a hard place here. Have either of you gotten any leads yet?" She looked from Courtney to Mark.

"We're still interviewing people, Captain."

She glared at Mark, and Courtney imagined she bared her teeth like a wolf.

"People or suspects? Wait, don't tell me, you don't have any suspects, do you? And please don't say Park Mugger in front of me. We are not even going there."

"Why not?" Mark asked. "Detective Lang pointed out some interesting correlations between the three murders and the Park Muggings."

"I don't want to hear it." She waved her hands. "The only correlation I will consider right now is that all three had been victimized previously and each had a disability of some sort. That seems like too much of a coincidence to me. Other than that, the victims were of different ages and genders and none of them seemed connected in any other way." She stood from her desk and walked over to the murder board on her wall.

"Hamilton had been deaf since birth. McCarver was blinded in an accident as a child. Fredericks, however, lost her arm in an accident less than a year ago."

Courtney winced as she looked at the crime scene photos beneath each name. Next to Agnes, Joe, and Gloria were regular shots, probably supplied by their families. They looked like before and after photos, before and after death. The thought chilled her. What bothered her most is that she recognized Gloria Fredericks. She and Bill had been involved in the investigation of the theft of her painting.

"I've already spoken with Detective Thompson," Sansone continued. "I want him in a more active role in this investigation. He seems to have more experience and sense than both of you." Courtney took objection to her comment, but she knew it would irk Mark even more. He had his eye on the vase of flowers on Sansone's desk. Flattery seemed to win Bill an edge over them.

"What do you mean a more active role?" Mark asked.

Sansone paused following his gaze to the flowers. She touched a petal of the pink roses. Friendship. It must've cost Bill a pretty penny to buy their captain's.

"I want Detective Thompson out in the field again. I understand he has limitations, but he's capable of handling them, and he won't be alone." She looked at Courtney. "I'm reassigning him as your partner. Mark will take over the evidence work until this case is solved."

Courtney felt her mouth drop open. So this was Bill's revenge on Mark.

"Wait a minute," Mark protested. "If you allow this, Captain, you will be putting both Detective Thompson and Detective Lang in jeopardy. How can she protect herself from danger if she has to watch out for a disabled man, too?"

"This isn't my sole decision, Detective Farrell. I've spoken to Detective Thompson's personal physician and Dr. Klein. They assure me it's safe and will also be of benefit to him."

"I bet it will," Mark muttered under his breath.

"Did you say something, Detective Farrell?"

Mark stood up. "I said, yes, Captain. It's fine. Are we switching offices, too?"

She nodded. "Yes. I think that would be best for the time being. You don't need to move everything, but please assist Detective Thompson with whatever he wants to bring with him. He's clearing out his desk now."

"I'm on it," Mark said. Courtney could hear the sarcasm in his voice. He strode out of the office, leaving Courtney alone with Sansone.

"I hope you understand this change, Detective Lang. You and Detective Thompson work well together. We're doing what's best for the department."

"Yes, Captain." Courtney forced a smile and then headed out the door. As she looked back, Sansone was sniffing her flowers. Courtney noticed they were her favorites.

# Chapter Ten

Mark came in carrying a bundle of files and dropped them on the desk. His face was red. "He's gloating, Court. I was this close to quitting." He pinched two fingers together.

"Mark, please. Calm down. Give Bill a chance. If it doesn't work out, Sansone will realize she's made a mistake."

"I don't believe it. You're on their side."

"There are no sides, Mark. We all work together. We're a team."

"You know what I think? I think you're happy about this. I know you still have feelings for him."

Before Courtney could deny the accusation, Bill came into her office with another pile of folders on his lap. "And if she does, Mark, what is it to you? She told me it's over between the two of you. Don't be a sore loser about it."

Courtney's heart leaped as she saw Mark ball his hands into fists. She was afraid he would punch Bill. Instead, he turned and faced the other detective. "You know what? I'm leaving early today. You can finish clearing out your desk. If you need help, ask your girlfriend or Sansone. You sure buttered her up to request this change."

Courtney was glad that Bill didn't respond. He watched as Mark walked past him to the door. At the door, Mark called back, "If there's anything of mine in the desk you need to move to make room for Detective Thompson's stuff, just throw it out, Courtney."

After Mark had gone, Bill said, "Sansone's not going to like his leaving early when we're in the middle of a case." He rolled to the desk and added the additional folders.

"I think you two need to have a discussion with Myra."

"I'm through with the shrink, Courtney. I'm adjusting fine, which is more than I can say for you and Detective Farrell."

"Bill, if we're all going to work together, you have to find a way to be more civil to Mark."

He paused, considering her comment. "I guess that's fair, but he has to man up and admit when he's wrong."

She decided it was useless to argue with Bill. Sansone had made her decision, and Courtney had no choice but to comply. She changed the subject. "Did Sansone give you an assignment for this afternoon?"

"Yes. She gave *us* an assignment. We'll be speaking with the man who found Fredericks dead in her house. I have the address in my phone, and Sansone had them equip a handicapped van for me, so you won't need to worry about lifting me in and out of the chair."

"Seems like you and Sansone have become buddies. I must say the flowers were very nice."

He smiled. "Thank you, Courtney. By the way, this is turning out to be a nice birthday for me."

It was then that she recalled the dinner with Bill and his brother that night. This new development would create a different atmosphere than she'd imagined.

***

The van that Sansone had ordered for Bill turned out to be quite accessible for his wheelchair. He was able to roll it up the lift that automatically lowered as the car doors opened. Courtney got behind the wheel. He had given her the address of the Peapod deliverer who was home on a personal day after having found Gloria Fredericks. She steered the van in that direction.

Greg Henderson was a retired banker in his sixties who had taken a part-time job at Peapod a year ago. He opened the door of his small home with a finger to his lips. "My wife is sleeping. I gave her some pills to relax her. She was so upset when I told her what happened. I should take some myself, but I don't think sedatives mix well with Scotch."

He gave Bill an odd look as he wheeled himself through the door. Courtney hadn't counted on the reaction of witnesses and suspects to the detective's disability.

"I'm Detective Thompson and this is my partner, Detective Lang," Bill introduced them, flashing his badge. He lingered on the word "partner."

"Please come in." The white-haired man led them into his living room, a plain room with photos of his family standing in frames on the end tables and displayed across the off-white walls. There were two sons posing with Henderson and his wife in various backgrounds—by a lake, on the beach, around a table laden with trimmings from a Thanksgiving meal.

"My two sons," Henderson said proudly observing Courtney's glances around the room. "They're both married now with children of their own." He walked to the couch. "Have a seat. I can make some coffee if you'd like. I might need some myself."

"No, please don't bother," Courtney said. Bill moved into an empty spot next to the couch. Henderson remained standing.

"This is a nightmare. I delivered to her on a weekly basis. She was so kind and always gave me a nice tip."

"Tell us what happened the day you found the body," Bill inquired.

Henderson ran a hand over his face. Courtney noticed it was spread with fine white hairs. "I tapped on the door as I usually do. Her doorbell was out of order. It had been that way for weeks. She said she was going to get a repairman to fix it, but I guess she hadn't gotten around to it." He swallowed. "When she didn't answer, I got a little concerned. She never missed a delivery."

"What did you do then?" Courtney prompted.

"I looked through the door. There was a peephole, so I could see in. I didn't notice anything out of order, so I kept on knocking. One knock was pretty hard, and the door swung open. I was surprised. People sometimes keep their doors open, but I hadn't expected it. I stepped in and called. Then I noticed that the place was messed up."

"What do you mean?" Bill had his hands folded in his lap, his attention on Henderson.

"Some stuff was scattered around. I was afraid someone broke in. I knew about her stolen painting and was worried she'd been robbed again."

Courtney wondered how friendly Fredericks had been with the Peapod deliverer for her to tell him her business, or maybe he'd found out through the newspaper story.

"Go on," Bill urged.

"I called again and then, maybe I shouldn't have, but I checked around the house." He paused, took a breath. "I found her in the bedroom lying face down on the floor, a tie around her neck. I knew she was dead. I didn't touch her. I knew I shouldn't. I watch crime shows with my wife. I know you shouldn't contaminate evidence. I called 911." He covered his face with his hands again. "I'm quitting my route. I gave notice to Peapod. I'll find a desk job somewhere or stay home with Lucy. The money was just for extras, anyway."

"I don't understand something. I've used Peapod occasionally when I haven't had time to shop, and they've always arrived in a white and green truck with their delivery service logo. Our captain didn't indicate that any

Peapod trucks were stolen, so I wonder why Ms. Fredericks let the man in to begin with."

Henderson glanced at Courtney. "I have no idea. As I said, I arrived after the, uh, crime."

"What time was this?" Bill asked. Courtney knew he'd already read the report that indicated time of death was around ten a.m. that morning, the same time she and Mark were interviewing Sanchez.

"I got there at eleven. When people place their Peapod orders, they receive a two-hour window for delivery. We were scheduled from ten to twelve today. I had a few houses before Ms. Fredericks."

"Did you notice anyone near the house when you got there, or did you see any occupied cars on the street?" Courtney knew Bill's questioning would be met with a negative response. An hour after strangling Fredericks, her killer wouldn't be hanging around.

"No. It was a quiet block. I didn't notice anything."

"Then, when you went into the house, you said it looked like it had been trashed."

"I didn't say that, Detective Thompson. There were a few things out of place, knocked over—the coffee table, a chair, but it wasn't a total wreck."

*Enough to indicate a struggle*, Courtney thought.

"I really can't tell you anything else. I'm sorry, but I'd rather not think about it anymore. It was an experience I'd rather forget."

"I understand," Bill said, "Unfortunately, a woman is dead, and you were the one who found her."

The Peapod driver's face paled. "I'm not a suspect, am I? God, she was a nice lady. I would never . . ."

Instead of consoling him that he wasn't under suspicion, Bill said, "There have been two other murders with the same M.O., Mr. Henderson. All three of the victims had a disability of some sort. We are investigating all leads."

"M.O.?" Henderson looked confused.

"Modus Operandi. That means the killer operated in the same way. The victims were all strangled."

Henderson's face still appeared ashen. "So awful. If anything comes back to me, I'll be sure to contact you."

"Thank you." Bill handed him his card.

***

Back in the van, Courtney said, "I hate to bring this up, Bill, but can I ask you why Sansone put you on this case? I don't think it's just because you brought her flowers."

In the rearview mirror, she could see his face in the back. His mouth turned up into a slight grin. "Maybe she feels I can identify with the victims and their families. Unless you have a disability yourself, you don't fully understand what it's like."

"I guess that makes sense, but it doesn't explain why you would be on the case. Did you consider it might put you in danger?"

"Sansone answered that question for you and Farrell. My doctors and Klein agree I'm fit enough to function in the field."

"That's not what I mean." She started the car and headed back toward the station. "If this killer they are calling the Handicapped Strangler is offing disabled people, wouldn't it be a risk for you to make yourself visible to him?" Before Bill could reply, Courtney realized that she had answered her own question. Sansone had assigned this case to Bill to ferret out the killer.

***

It felt strange and yet familiar for Courtney to be sharing her office with her old partner again. The space seemed smaller because Bill had to maneuver his wheelchair through it. His files were still piled on her desk where Mark had dropped them before taking the rest of the day off. She wondered if he would accept Sansone's decision or if he was angry enough to submit his resignation. She hoped not. This was only a temporary arrangement. As much as she once enjoyed having Bill as a partner, it wasn't just the physical change in him that had made things different. It had been her experience working with Mark. Bill was smart, but Mark was wise. He complemented her in ways Bill never had.

She opened Mark's desk drawer to see what she should move to his office. She wasn't going to throw stuff out as he'd suggested. Bill watched her work. She noticed his face seemed a bit strained and wondered if the outing had tired him.

"I think I may make this an early day," he said. "Sansone already okayed my leaving early for my birthday. Tomorrow, we're scheduled to speak to the parents."

Courtney knew he was referring to the Fredericks. That interview would be tougher than the one with Henderson.

"That's fine, Bill. I'm just making room for your stuff. I'll write up the report from our interview and give it to Sansone before I leave."

"Thank you." He wheeled over to her. "One last thing, Court. I want to apologize for my behavior toward Farrell. He just pushes my buttons sometimes. I also would hate to see you hurt by him."

"Bill, please. I already told you it's over between me and Mark. I know you wanted to work this case to prove yourself to me, and Sansone sees it as an opportunity to catch the Handicapped Strangler, but this rivalry between you and Mark can only end badly. I care about both of you—as friends and co-workers, nothing more."

Bill rolled back. "I'm not too sure about that. I think it's what you're telling yourself."

With that, he left the office.

Courtney sat there a few minutes pondering his words and then got back to work clearing the desk. As she emptied Mark's drawer, something small fell out of it. She recognized the evidence bag, but how had it gotten there? Evidence was rarely removed from the Evidence Room. She picked up the bag to see what it contained. It was the black fiber found at the McCarver crime scene, the one that was identified as a wool hat but which she contended was part of the Park Mugger's ski mask. What should she do with it? There must be a reason Mark had it in his drawer. She could return it to Evidence or bring it along with his other papers to his new office. She decided to do neither. Instead, she placed it in her purse with the intention of asking Mark about it when she saw him again.

She finished her work on the desk, brought Mark's files into Bill's office where she filled the drawers he had emptied, and then delivered the interview report to Sansone. The woman gave her a curt nod as she took the papers Courtney handed her and went back to typing into her computer.

Courtney took a deep breath as she left the building. It was dark and cold out with the scent of approaching snow in the air, but she welcomed the change from the overheated, fluorescent lit police station. As she started her car, she checked the clock and saw that it was after six. She was scheduled to be at Bill and Rick's house at seven. She had just enough time to pick up Italian food and a birthday cake on her way. She thought about a card and gift but decided they weren't appropriate under the circumstances. The meal and dessert would be gift enough. She wasn't looking forward to this surprise party after the events of the day and her talk with Bill, but she couldn't back out of it now.

# Chapter Eleven

She stopped at Donatelli's, Bill's favorite family-owned Italian restaurant where they used to dine before he was shot. The restaurant had a takeout counter in front, and booths and tables in the back for diners. Donna, the red-headed waitress, was still there. She recognized Courtney immediately as she entered. "Well, hello, stranger. Where's Mr. Bill?"

Courtney realized Donna didn't know about the shooting despite all the coverage in the newspaper last summer. She decided not to fill her in.

"Hi, Donna. He's at home. I'm picking up some food for him for his birthday."

The waitress smiled. "That's sweet. Are you two tying the knot anytime soon?"

The question made Courtney wonder why Bill hadn't chosen the intimate restaurant for his proposal instead of the park. Things might've turned out much differently if he had. "No. I'm afraid not. We're just friends now."

Donna shook her head, sending a few red curls bobbing. "Too bad. Well, it's nice of you to get him a birthday dinner. What will it be? His usual lasagna?"

"That'll be fine. Make it three of those. His brother will be eating with us."

Donna jotted on her pad and then went back to the kitchen with the order. Courtney took a seat in a nearby booth to wait. She glanced absently at a plastic menu on the table as memories flooded her mind. Bill had taken her here for her birthday last May. He'd gotten a table in the private back room and ordered a bottle of wine. He'd even hired the restaurant's violinist to entertain them.

"Happy birthday, Courtney," he'd said, raising a glass of the wine.

She raised her glass, and he brought his to meet hers. "To many more happy years."

They clinked glasses and then he reached into his pocket. "I have a little gift for you, my love."

As he brought a small wrapped present from his pocket, she saw the happiness on his face. "I think you're more excited about my birthday than I am, Bill."

"I love giving you gifts. I love making you happy."

She opened the box. A pair of emerald earring studs sat against a white velvet lined jewelry box.

"Oh, Bill. These are beautiful."

"They're your birthstone. Put them on."

She removed her pearl earrings and exchanged them for the emeralds.

He reached across the table and took her hand as the violinist played a romantic melody.

Courtney was brought back to reality as Donna returned to the counter with the packaged lasagna meals. She rang up the order, and Courtney paid with her credit card and added a five-dollar bill to the tip jar.

"Thank you, my dear. Please bring Bill next time. I can give you the private room when it isn't used for parties." She winked.

Courtney felt her stomach drop. She made a non-committal comment, took the bags, and left the restaurant.

Her next stop was the bakery. Luckily, she and Bill had never gone there together. She selected his favorite Black Forest cake and asked the baker if she wouldn't mind writing, "Happy Birthday, Bill" on it. She also added a few yellow flowers along with the white icing.

Courtney placed the cake box on the passenger seat and the brown paper dinner bags in the back seat and started driving toward Rick's house. It was nearly seven, so she wouldn't be late. She remembered the way even though she hadn't been there since she helped Bill move in six months ago. The house was the one in which the brothers had grown up. Bill had moved to his own apartment several years ago, allowing his younger brother to stay in the house even though their parents had left it in both their names after they'd died from cancer less than a year apart. Bill told her once, when he'd explained this, that he liked his privacy and, rather than sell the house to strangers, he would prefer Rick live in it until one of them married. It turned out Bill came home sooner than that.

It wasn't a large home, but carrying her packages up the walk, she realized it had a certain charm. The ranch featured a front porch, large bay windows that looked out from the kitchen, and a sleeping dog rolled up on the welcome mat. "Hey, boy, what are you doing out here in the cold?" Courtney asked. The dog, a mix between a German shepherd and a terrier, looked up at her with warm brown eyes. She recalled Rick had a dog named Rufus.

As she tapped on the door, not sure if Rick had already sprung the "surprise" on Bill, the dog gathered next to her. She patted his scruffy head as she waited. Rick answered a few minutes later with a smile on his face.

"Hi, Rick. I've brought dinner and your dog."

"Thanks, Courtney. I forgot he was out there. He really loves to sit on the porch even in the cold. I told Bill we're having someone over to dinner, but he doesn't know who. Come on in." He opened the door to allow her and Rufus to enter. The dog ran in first, shaking himself in the entry hall.

Courtney hadn't seen the house since it was converted for accessibility. She'd noted the handicapped ramp on the other side of the porch, but now she saw that some additional work was done to accommodate Bill, one of the reasons he moved back in with Rick. There had been a hefty settlement from his insurance that covered a policeman injured in the line of duty. Some of that money went toward these modifications. Bill had also told her that he'd given Rick some of it to start his website business.

After Rick placed the cake in the refrigerator and she helped him set the table and lay out the food, she asked where Bill was.

"He's in his room. I'll go get him. Have a seat, and thanks again. He's been a bit depressed lately. This will cheer him up." She thought Sansone's reassigning him had already done that.

A few minutes later, Bill wheeled himself into the kitchen. Rick had left a spot open for his chair. He didn't seem surprised when he saw her. "Hello, Courtney. Nice to see you in, what, three hours?" He glanced at the kitchen clock over the bay window. Looking toward it, she saw that a few flakes were falling outside.

"I wanted to wish you a happy birthday," she said. "The food's from Donatelli's, and I also picked up a cake."

"How sweet." He glanced at Rick. "Nice of you both to set this up."

Rick took three cans of Budweiser out of the fridge, placed them on the table, and sat down next to Bill. "I should've gotten some wine, so we could toast your thirty-secondth year, but I guess the beer will have to do." He opened his can and poured its contents into a glass that he passed to Bill. Then he poured some for himself and glanced at Courtney. "Join us?"

"I'll just have water, thanks." Courtney didn't care for beer.

"I'll get it," Bill offered, taking her glass-to the sink, which she noted was low enough for him to reach the spouts.

"Thanks," she said when he brought the glass back after adding ice.

"Let's have our toast," Rick proposed. He raised his glass. "To my brother. I hope this year is a good one for you."

Courtney and Bill both raised their glasses, but Bill's expression had changed. He'd lost his smile.

The rest of the evening seemed forced. Rick tried to tell some jokes, but Bill remained quiet. During the singing of "Happy Birthday" when Rick encouraged Bill to blow out the single candle he found in a drawer to make a wish because Courtney had forgotten to bring any along with her, Bill said, "I don't believe in wishes, but I'd like to have dessert." Rick moved the cake as close as possible to the edge of the table, and Bill blew out the candle in one breath.

Rick and Courtney applauded, then Courtney cut the cake, serving the men and then herself. She was looking forward to ending the night when Rick said, "Before you go, maybe you'd like to see my office." Courtney thought he was asking because he wanted to speak to her alone. She nodded. "Sure."

Bill said, "I'm a bit tired, so I'll be going to my room. I brought some files home from the station to look through before bed."

"You shouldn't be working on your birthday," Courtney said.

"It's what I want to do, and I believe birthdays are for doing what you want."

She hadn't meant to anger him. "Of course. See you tomorrow. I hope you enjoyed dinner."

He gave her a half smile. "It was nice. Good night." Then he wheeled himself down the hall. Courtney couldn't help but feel peeved because he hadn't even thanked her for bringing the food and cake.

As Rick led Courtney to his office, a door on the left side of the hall, Rufus came bounding after them.

She gasped as she entered the room into which Rick led her. Although tiny, it featured two, state-of-the-art computers in workstations. One was a PC; the other a Mac. There was a 3D printer, a large screen, and audio equipment. Books on graphic design, Photoshop, and Website development lined the built-in library shelves. A desk which held a third computer had a black leather rolling chair in front of it where Rick could sit in comfort.

"Wow!" Courtney exclaimed. "You have quite a nice office."

He smiled, and she couldn't help but notice his freckles. His boyish grin and his height added to the impression of a young boy with his toys. At twenty-eight, Rick was four years younger than Bill but could almost pass for his son. Even though Courtney knew the experience which disabled him had also aged him, Bill still seemed more mature than his younger brother.

"Have a look around, Courtney. I'm indebted to Bill for this setup. He's turned his delinquent brother into a businessman."

"He only gave you the tools," she pointed out, "and you were kind enough to have your home adjusted to meet his needs."

"It's the least I could do." He pointed toward a chair next to the desk. "Take a seat. I think you wanted to talk to me about Bill. The evening seemed to have turned out well. He seemed less stressed. He told me earlier that you're working with him again. That's great. Are you guys, you know, back together again personally?"

"No."

She watched as disappointment flickered across Rick's face, but it was only momentary. "That's too bad. I think you two were good together."

"I'd really rather not go into that." Courtney glanced around the room. She could see some website designs on the monitors. "Do you like designing websites?" She decided to change the subject.

"Beats stealing the money. Whoops, sorry. I forget you're a cop."

"Don't worry. Bill told me about your wild days. I'm glad you're earning money the respectable way now."

"I owe that to my older brother. As you said, he gave me the tools."

"I don't mean to intrude, Rick, but the reason I wanted to sit down with the two of you tonight was not just to celebrate Bill's birthday, but to try to iron out the ill will he has toward Detective Farrell. I didn't get the chance to do that, but maybe you can have a word with him."

Rick grinned again. "I doubt that would help. My brother is quite stubborn. The only reason he moved in with me was because he basically had no choice. It would've been very difficult for him to stay alone in his apartment. I think he could handle it now, but not when he first came out of the hospital. You remember."

"Yes. I do." Courtney recalled the difficulty Bill had adjusting to his disability in the beginning.

Rick shrugged. "I think the main issue between Bill and this other detective is not that they don't get along, it's you."

"I'm aware of that." Courtney knew Bill was jealous, but he didn't have a right to be, not since Bill had let her go without a fight, and she'd now broken off with Mark. But Myra had suggested that Courtney should've been the one to put up an argument about Bill ending their relationship in the first place.

"What I suggest is to have them work it out themselves. I think you getting in the middle is a mistake."

Courtney knew he was right. "Okay. I'll let them duel it out themselves."

Rick laughed. "Don't worry. They won't shoot one another."

*Bad choice of words*, Courtney thought, remembering her dream. "Let's hope not."

# Chapter Twelve

Courtney slept well that night with Oliver rolled up in a beige ball next to her. No nightmares or dreams of any kind intruded her slumber. In the morning, after she'd fed the cat and sat down to coffee, she recalled that today was her first full day as Bill's partner. She wondered if Mark would be at work and if Rick was right that he and Bill could iron things out. She resolved to stay out of it. She was no longer romantically involved with either man. She had to keep her working relationships purely platonic.

The phone rang. It was Bill. "Courtney, thanks for last night. It was a nice surprise. I just called to remind you about our interview with Jessica and Ronald Fredericks."

Courtney had forgotten that they were scheduled to speak with Gloria's parents that day. "Hi, Bill. I'm glad you enjoyed your birthday meal and cake. Thanks for the reminder about the interview. Are we meeting at the station first?"

"Yes. Our appointment isn't until eleven, and I have a few things to go over with Sansone before we leave. I did some work last night, and I think I have a suspect."

"What? Who?" Was Courtney hearing right?

"I'll fill you in later." He clicked off before she could comment.

*** 

Bill and Sansone were behind closed doors in her office for a half hour. When he finally came out, Bill said, "Sansone is calling a meeting with the department. Can you tell everyone to meet in her office at ten? It should be over before we have to leave for the Fredericks.'"

Courtney spread the word to upraised eyebrows and questions. She knew the meeting probably involved whatever Bill had dug up last night in the files and what he had mentioned about a suspect.

When she got to Mark's office, she knocked on his door. She knew he was there but was keeping to himself. He hadn't even gotten coffee from the staff lounge but had brought in a cup from Starbucks on his way.

"Come in," he called. When he saw her in the doorway, he concentrated on the papers before him. She recalled the evidence she still had in her bag and wondered if she should mention it to him. She decided this wasn't a good time. She had to see how he was dealing with their break up, both working and personal.

"Sansone has called a meeting in her office at ten." She kept her voice cool, professional.

Mark looked up from the papers, his blue eyes quizzical behind his reading glasses, a strand of dark hair falling across his forehead. "Do you know what it's about?"

She hesitated. "No, but Bill hinted that they may have a suspect in the Handicapped Strangler case."

His face remained passive. Then he checked his watch. "I see. Okay, I'll be there."

As she turned to go, he called out to her. "Courtney."

"Yes, Mark."

"I'm sorry for how I behaved yesterday. It was childish. I'm sure Sansone's decision is for the best. Bill is an excellent detective. I have to keep my personal feelings objective when it comes to you."

She nodded. "Yes, I'm planning to do that, too."

He smiled. "Thanks also for bringing my files here. I'm glad you didn't toss them."

\*\*\*

They gathered in Sansone's office. Bill was already parked by her desk as Courtney and the others entered. Mark came in last. He stood on the opposite side of the room from Courtney. She regretted that. She had hoped they could salvage their friendship, but she felt better when he smiled across at her.

On Sansone's crime board where the photos of the victims were posted, there was a new photo above which the captain had written in red marker, "Suspect: Harrison Shride." Courtney gazed at a stocky, white-haired man with a youthful face as Sansone cleared her throat to open the meeting. She looked around the room at the other detectives and officers as she spoke. Courtney noticed her flower arrangement was starting to wilt.

"Thank you for coming. I'll make this brief as Detectives Lang and Thompson have an appointment at eleven." Her eyes moved toward Bill and then to Courtney.

"Thanks to Detective Thompson we have a suspect in the Handicapped Strangler case."

There were loud murmurs around the room. "Be quiet a moment. Let me fill you all in. Actually, I think it's best if Detective Thompson explains." She glanced again at Bill, who eagerly picked up her story.

"Harrison Shride is a lawyer whom I found had a connection with each of the victims. He had drawn up Agnes McCarver's will last month. He was also hired by Joseph Hamilton's parents to represent him in a case of DWI a few years ago, the one and only time it seems he ever broke the law." He paused and then continued watching the reactions of those attending the meeting. "Shride was the Fredericks' family lawyer, too."

Carter Jackson, one of the younger officers who habitually questioned everything, asked, "Just because this guy had a connection to the vics doesn't mean he killed them. What proof do you have?"

"I haven't finished." Bill looked slightly angered. He drew in a breath. "Once I found that he had dealt with McCarver, Hamilton, and Fredericks, I dug a little deeper into Shride's past. It seems he was given up for adoption by his parents who were both disabled and couldn't cope with caring for him. Before he went to law school, he worked in a facility for the disabled and was charged with assaulting a resident. His adopted father, also a lawyer, managed to have those charges cleared, but he obviously couldn't erase them."

Sansone nodded. "Very good work, Thompson, but that's still not enough evidence to link him to the crimes. I want you and Lang to pay a visit to Mr. Shride's law office after you see the Fredericks, ask him a few questions, and check his whereabouts on the dates of the three murders. The rest of you"—she glanced around the room— "keep this quiet. I don't want the press to know anything." The murmurs died down as the other officers shook their heads in agreement. "I'm keeping my fingers crossed that this is a good lead. The meeting is adjourned."

As the officers filed out, Mark approached the desk. "Before you two leave"—he indicated Courtney and Bill who were still by Sansone— "I want to volunteer to interview Shride. You'll be busy with the Fredericks'. It'll save time."

"Absolutely not," Sansone said. "Remember, you're on desk duty, Detective Farrell."

Courtney thought she caught the hint of a smile at the corner of Bill's mouth. She felt sorry for Mark as he made another plea to Sansone. "Can't you make an exception this one time for the sake of the case?"

Sansone pursed her lips and remained resolute. "I'm afraid that's not possible. Detective Thompson and Detective Lang will speak with Shride. That's my final word on the matter. Now if you don't mind, I have work to get back to, and I suggest you get back to yours, as well."

She turned to face Bill and Courtney. "Good luck with your interviews, Detectives."

# Chapter Thirteen

Behind the wheel, driving to the hotel where the Fredericks were staying, Courtney said, "I think Sansone is being a bit rough on Mark. He's clearly bored being confined to the desk, and he's a good cop. He could be of use on this case."

"He'll be of use," Bill said. "There's lots of paperwork for him to manage."

"He didn't go to the police academy to push papers."

"Neither did I."

"Is that what this is about, Bill? Revenge on Mark for not being disabled or for having dated me?"

"Maybe both." At least he admitted the truth. "But Courtney, I didn't tie Sansone's hands on this. It was her choice."

"No, you gave her flowers."

He smiled. "Maybe I should get you some."

She remembered the lovely bouquets he always had delivered for Valentine's Day, her birthday, and the anniversary of the day they'd met which was coming up in a few days. She hadn't forgotten that. When she first started ten years ago at Baxter, she was paired up with a veteran officer who retired three years ago. That's when Sansone assigned Bill as her new partner. They'd clicked right away, but it took a year before he'd built up the nerve to ask her out on an official date, although they'd spent plenty of nights working late together over pizza and beer.

"No thanks." She brought her mind back to the present. She didn't mean it to sound unkind, but to her ears it did. "I'm sorry, Bill. I know how you feel." They were almost at the Hilton.

"You can't possibly know how I feel," he said in a low voice that seemed to seethe with anger, or maybe it was hurt.

*\*\*\**

The interview with Gloria's parents didn't reveal anything new. The mother, Jessica, sat through the whole discussion with her face in a handkerchief as if she was crying, but Courtney could tell they were false tears. During the short times she raised her head, her gray eyes were clear and not even her mascara was smudged.

The father, Paul Fredericks IV, was another matter. He met each question with an angry response, but Courtney got the impression he was madder at his daughter for being killed than at them for asking about it. It was also obvious he'd wanted a son instead of a daughter and blamed his wife for failing to deliver a child of the right sex. Courtney couldn't believe, in this day and age, that such a chauvinist pig existed. Of course, he masked it well.

"I told her it was dangerous to move out here all alone, but women, they don't listen." He paced around, hands in his pockets. They were in the hotel lounge. Bill thought it would be easier speaking with them there than in their room, but he was wrong. Although few guests were nearby, Paul's loud voice drifted toward the front desk where people were coming and going as they checked in and out.

"I thought the accident would change her mind. It was a terrible thing. She was so talented, could've achieved so much more. If it happened in New York, I would've had the best surgeon repair her arm. If she'd moved back, I had the names of some top physical therapists who might've been able to help." He turned to his wife, who still had her face in the handkerchief, and spoke about her in third person. "Jessie should've tried harder to talk her into coming home, never leaving at all. Girls listen to their mothers."

"I don't think this is your wife's fault or yours," Courtney said. "We're trying to find the person who murdered your daughter. Do you know anyone who would want to harm her?"

"How the hell should I know that? She kept to herself. Never had a lot of friends at home, and I doubt she made many in this backwater town. But no one hated her either. She was lovely, smart, talented. I gave her everything, but she turned it all away, wanted to be independent. Look what it got her."

Courtney knew the real reason Gloria had left her parents. It wasn't just for independence. Her father was a controlling and domineering man, and her mother was a spineless shell of a woman.

Bill glanced at his watch. "We really don't have much more time to spend here, but there's one thing we need to know. What was Gloria's relationship with your lawyer, Harrison Shride?"

Fredericks stopped pacing. "Shride? What does he have to do with this?"

"We don't know, but we found that he was connected to all three of the victims who were killed recently, including your daughter."

"That's insane. Harrison and I are friends. We go golfing every Friday on Long Island. You don't think he's a suspect in these, what are they calling them, Handicapped Stranglings?"

"We're just checking things out for now. Did Shride know your daughter?"

Fredericks remained stationary. "He met her a few times. He helped after her accident, of course. That's what lawyers do." Courtney noticed he seemed fidgety, afraid of giving the wrong response.

"Shride lives in Westport, only a few miles from Baxter," Bill said.

"Yes. He commuted to the City each day. I had to give him credit for that. I'm retired now, but I had the privilege of working from home when I was younger. I still put in grueling fifteen-hour days practicing." He looked down at his hands. Courtney noticed they were the tapered fingers of a pianist. "People think a musician's life is all glamour, but it's sweat and tears, too. Maybe Gloria wasn't prepared for that. She was too pampered, too spoiled. Her mother and I did her an injustice, and now we're paying." Courtney saw real tears in the man's eyes and wondered if, despite his demeanor, maybe he was taking this harder than his wife.

***

Courtney felt uncomfortable driving the van into New York City, but it wasn't because of the crowded streets, crazy drivers, or the tunnels and tolls. It was because she was aware of Bill in the back.

She tried to make conversation, but it wasn't easy. His answers were flat and succinct. It was like talking to Oliver, only the cat seemed to respond in a warmer way. Finally, she resorted to asking about the upcoming interview. "So, do you really think the killer is Shride? What tipped you off?"

Bill sighed. "Sansone didn't want this publicized, but I received an anonymous call saying I should investigate Harrison Shride's connection to the Handicapped Strangler victims. As far as his being guilty, I don't know. I hope so. This case has got Sansone in a tizzy. I'd like to see it solved."

"It would be nice to end the killings, too." She hadn't meant to sound sarcastic.

When Bill went silent again, Courtney decided to change the subject. "Look, I know we haven't been on the best terms since, well, you know. It wasn't easy for me. You put up a wall, but maybe I should've been more persistent in breaking it down."

"Courtney." The way he said her name had her look back at him in the rearview mirror. The edge was gone from his tone, replaced by something else that frightened her more.

Whatever Bill was about to say was interrupted by a horn blast as a black Honda cut her off. "What the . . . oh, these City drivers. They make me insane."

"I recall you were a pretty crazy driver yourself in the day."

She let that remark go as they pulled up at the law office of Shride and Knowles. It was in a prime Manhattan location and was located on the top floor of a gleaming ten-story glass building.

After finding parking in the underground lot, Courtney waited for the ramp to lower and for Bill to roll out of the van before she joined him. She had to resist the impulse to push him.

Snow had started to fall as they'd entered the City, and there was already a light dusting of it on the ground. Unlike the holiday warmth that spirited New York in December, January gave the place a cold and distant air. Such a difference a month could make. But then, again, people could change overnight. Bill was back to his unemotional self as he scooted toward the handicapped ramp that led from the parking garage to the building.

They rode the glass elevator up to the offices of Shride and Knowles. Men and women in business suits got off on various floors on the way up. All the floors looked similar, so Courtney had to keep an eye on the elevator listing, although it featured a device that announced each stop.

When the mechanical voice said, "Top Floor. Offices of Shride and Knowles," they were the last ones in the elevator. When the doors opened, she waited for Bill to wheel out and then followed him down the marble hall. Green plants she couldn't identify stood in pots by the stairway and in areas that featured couches and other seats. At the end of the hall, they came to a door labeled, "Shride and Knowles, Esq. Attorneys-At-Law."

It was then that Courtney realized she hadn't asked Bill if Shride was expecting them. "Do we have an appointment, Bill?"

"No. Sansone thought it would be best to catch him unaware. Go on in, I see the secretary at her desk."

Courtney stepped around him and opened the door, holding it for him to enter. The woman at the desk, in her fifties with rust-colored hair that matched the frames of her glasses, looked over at them. Her canned greeting did not consist of a smile. "How may I help you?"

"We're here to see Mr. Shride," Bill said, flashing his badge.

The woman lifted a thin, tweezed brow over her glasses. "I'm afraid he's in a meeting, but you can speak with Mr. Knowles if you wait a few minutes." She indicated the leather seating area behind yet another anonymous plant.

"That won't work, ma'am. We need to speak to Mr. Shride. We're willing to wait until he's available if he can fit us in."

Courtney prayed they hadn't made the trip for nothing. So much for not making an appointment.

"He's with a client right now, but if you don't mind waiting, I can let you know when he's free."

"Thank you." Bill wheeled himself by the plant and gestured for Courtney to have a seat. There was a stack of magazines on a nearby table, but she hesitated to take one.

After they'd waited a few minutes, a tall, thin man with a sandy-colored beard flecked with gray and a sparse head of hair that looked like it had appeared on an advertisement for men's hair color came out of a back room and approached the desk. The lawyer's face, despite his hair loss and premature gray, was that of a man in his early thirties. "Deirdre, do I have any messages?" He looked toward Courtney and Bill. "Are they here to see me?"

"No, Mr. Knowles. They're waiting for Mr. Shride."

He walked toward them. Recognizing that they were officers, he said, "Maybe I can help. I'm Jonathan Knowles, Harrison Shride's partner. He's tied up at the moment, but I'll be happy to assist you. Please step into my office." He waved toward the hall.

"We're here to see Mr. Shride," Bill persisted. "We don't mind waiting."

"Very well." He was about to turn when Courtney called out to him.

"Wait! Mr. Knowles, do you have access to your partner's appointment calendar?"

"No, but Deirdre, Ms. Miles, has that information. She keeps our schedules."

Bill gave Courtney a questioning glance, but she continued. "We need to check some dates."

"No problem. Mr. Shride should be free soon. If there's anything I can help with, just let Ms. Miles know." He walked back down the hall, and Courtney went to the desk. The secretary had tapped some keys on her computer, and Courtney assumed she'd brought up the online calendar for the lawyers' appointments.

"What dates did you need me to check?" she asked.

Courtney took out her pad on which she'd jotted the dates and times of the three murders. "We need to know if Mr. Shride was at the office during these times." She passed the pad to the secretary.

Bill came over, so he could be included in the discussion. Courtney wondered if he was upset she was taking the initiative in the questioning.

Miles's eyes moved back and forth from the pad to the computer screen. After paging up and down a few times through the screens, she handed the pad back to Courtney. "Mr. Shride was present on all these dates."

"Are you sure?" Bill asked. "Could he have left the office at any time?"

"I suppose it's possible, but he was booked pretty solid on those dates with clients. Sometimes Mr. Knowles fills in for him. They're partners, you know."

So they really should've asked Jonathan Knowles. Before they could ask to see him, another man came to the reception area whom Courtney recognized from his photo, but he looked younger than that image. He was stockily built, with a gray suit hugging his middle. Unlike his partner, Shride's thick hair was completely white, at odds with his age. "Sorry to keep you waiting, officers. Mr. Knowles tells me you need my help with something." He extended his hand for a shake. Courtney noticed no client exited with him, so that may have been an excuse to delay their visit. Also, Shride eyed Bill with a curious look as if he couldn't fathom a detective in a wheelchair.

Courtney shook his hand quickly and then he bent over to shake Bill's. "Please come to my office," he invited, leading them down the hall.

As soon as they had a seat in his opulent office that looked down upon the City through large shining glass windows where snowflakes were gathering, the lawyer's attitude changed. His friendliness was replaced with a wary expression. He closed the door behind them and sat behind his desk, swiveling his leather padded chair, steepling his fingers and gazing at them. "Before we begin, I want you both to be aware that I don't represent myself and will not be questioned without my lawyer present."

Courtney caught the tone of defensiveness she'd seen many times in guilty suspects. Bill said, "This is not an interrogation, sir. We just need some information. If we feel we should pursue this further, we'll call you in to our offices."

"I believe my secretary already gave you what you need." His eyes had turned hard. "I'm a busy man and don't have the time to play games with people who haven't booked an appointment with me."

Courtney was about to object that those rules didn't apply to the police, but Bill replied, "Sorry to inconvenience you. We'll certainly make an appointment next time. Let's go, Detective Lang."

As they exited, Shride remained at his desk. "There will be no need for another appointment. Have a good day, officers."

# Chapter Fourteen

Bill was silent as he rolled out of the building and toward the parking lot. Courtney found it hard to keep pace with him. She thought he was in a hurry for them to get back to Connecticut, but after she'd started up the van and lowered the ramp and he'd boarded, he said to her, "You want to grab some lunch somewhere before we head back and discuss what happened back there?"

She dusted some snow from her coat. "I'm not sure, Bill. It's starting to accumulate. I don't want us to get stuck here."

"Don't worry. It's just a flurry. I checked the weather on my phone."

She knew he was right, but she still hesitated. Her rumbling stomach made the decision. It was already after two, and she hadn't had a bite since a quick breakfast of coffee and toast with a dab of margarine. "Where do you have in mind?"

"We'll find a place. Preferably one with handicapped parking." He smiled, and she saw the touch of snow around his lips that had fallen from his hair. She had a flashback of them last December trudging through ankle-deep snow outside Radio City Music Hall where Bill had surprised her with tickets to the Christmas show. They were looking for a place to eat afterwards and found a small restaurant not far from Rockefeller Center that was surprisingly uncrowded despite the tasty food and atmospheric décor. They'd spent a happy hour there talking and eating. As it grew dark, they visited the lit-up tree where he'd embraced and kissed her. They'd strolled the City at night viewing the holiday window displays in some of the stores on the way back to the subway, and then caught the train where they rode home immersed in each other and cuddling in the only unoccupied seat.

Bill must've had the same memory because he added, a bit wistfully, "Sorry we can't do more walking like we used to, but the parking tabs will be on Baxter, and subways and trains are not the best modes of transport for those in wheelchairs."

It turned out they were lucky again by finding another small, uncrowded place that featured parking around the corner. The waitress, a young woman toting an earring through her nose and blue streaks in her short hair, made room for Bill at a table near the lit fireplace. She pulled away the chair to accompany his wheelchair. She then placed two menus on the table, smiled through braces, and left them to take an order from a nearby table.

Courtney tried to relax, but the fire brought a traumatic memory. She looked away and focused on the floor-to-ceiling windows instead. Despite Bill's optimistic view of the weather, the snow outside was piling up.

Bill checked the menu. "Glad Baxter will pick up the tab on this, too. A cheeseburger for twenty dollars. If the department wasn't paying, I would've taken you to McDonalds."

She smiled. "Save the receipt. Sansone is strict about that."

"So, what was your take on Shride?" He placed his menu upside down on the table. Courtney had decided on the chicken Caesar salad that matched the price of the cheeseburger. They were both the cheapest items listed. She placed her menu on top of his and looked across at him. "I was going to ask you the same question."

"Ladies first."

She was glad he was being polite. "Okay. I think he's hiding something."

"I agree. I hate dealing with lawyers. Some are good liars, but he wasn't."

"It's strange how they both look older than their years," Courtney said. "Did you notice that?"

"People age in different ways and for different reasons." Bill could've been talking about himself and how the shooting had added years to his appearance.

The waitress returned to take their orders and placed two tall glasses of water in front of them along with a small basket of rolls and sesame sticks. She inquired if they wanted anything else, a drink first or an appetizer. They declined.

After the waitress left, Courtney changed the subject. "It's starting to get heavier out there. I think we should head back as soon as we're through with lunch."

Bill agreed. "I guess the weathermen are wrong again." He looked across Courtney's shoulder to the windows. "I still don't think we need to rush. The flakes look thin."

"Easy for you to say. You're not driving." She regretted the words once they'd left her mouth.

"I could, you know. The van is equipped with hand controls. You would just need to assist me out of the chair."

"It's okay, Bill. I don't mind driving. Like you said, the roads are still clear enough."

She felt bad about the look that crossed his face. *He really does want to drive*, she thought and felt like she'd let him down again.

The food came a little while later. Even though her stomach started speaking again at its arrival, she had a hard time tasting anything. Bill made up for the two of them by cleaning his plate of burger and fries.

"I have a suggestion."

She pushed her half-eaten salad aside. "About what, Bill?"

"Driving back. What if we stay at a hotel tonight, tell Sansone the roads were too tricky, and add the cost to Baxter's tab?"

She found the idea plausible but thought of all the reasons it wouldn't work. "What if the snow is worse tomorrow? What if Sansone wants our report today?"

"If the snow is worse tomorrow, we stay another day courtesy of the Baxter P.D. If Sansone wants our report, which is scanty, we call or email her. I have a place in mind." His eyes lit up. He seemed sold on his own idea and happy about it. Before she could issue another argument, he continued. "I was thinking of the place we stayed for our anniversary last year."

Courtney gulped. Was it a coincidence, or had he remembered their anniversary was only days away? Last January, they had spent a weekend at the Park Lane Hotel in their honeymoon suite. He had joked that it was fun pretending to be married. A few months later, he'd proposed right before taking a bullet in the line of duty.

"That might not be a good idea."

"C'mon, Court. For old time's sake."

"We would need separate rooms."

"Certainly, but can they be connecting?"

"I guess that would be okay." She couldn't squash his enthusiasm.

He raised an eyebrow. "You don't think a disabled man would jump you when he hardly gets out of his wheelchair without help?"

"Bill, please." The busboy had arrived and cleared their table. The waitress followed on his heels and tossed the check on the table with a smile. Bill slid his credit card into the payment wallet along with a nice tip that Courtney knew Sansone wouldn't cover.

As the waitress walked away pocketing the money and card, Courtney said, "Sansone isn't going to like this, Bill, and it's possible there won't be any rooms available on such short notice."

"Stop worrying, Court. Screw Sansone, and I'm sure there are plenty of rooms on the off season after the holiday travelers have gone home."

They ended up on the third floor of Park Lane in a room directly adjacent from the elevator. When Bill flashed his badge for ID, the woman at the reservations desk said they were in luck that a handicapped room was available with a connecting room next door.

"See, Court. This is our lucky day," he said, as he opened the door using the card key. The slot was conveniently on waist level, so he only had to slide up to it. But when it turned green, Courtney had to help him push the heavy door open.

"Look at this," he exclaimed, eyeing the interior as Courtney switched on the lights. There was a neatly made king-sized bed. A control sat on it that activated the large screen TV set in the wall. The curtains of the large window were not yet drawn, so the falling flakes outside framed a lovely view against the darkening city. The bathroom had a roll-in tub.

"Let's go see your room," he said, moving toward the inner door. Since it was only for the night, Courtney didn't mind it being half the size as Bill's and containing a twin bed, nor the fact it had no window. But as he wheeled around the room, Bill asked, "Are you sure you don't want to bunk with me? There's plenty of space in the king."

She gave him a look, and he laughed. "Only kidding. I'm going to call the office and let them know that we're stranded here tonight."

She nodded. "Good idea." Then she had a thought. "I don't even have a toothbrush with me."

"I saw a small shop downstairs when we came in if you want to go pick up some sundries for us. Charge it to the room, and the bill will go to Baxter."

She hated putting more money on the department's tab, but there were some things she needed. "Okay. I'll be right back."

\*\*\*

When Courtney returned, Bill was sitting in his chair looking out the window at the snow.

"I got you a few things," she said, and he turned around. She opened the bag and placed some Kit Kat bars on his side table. She had noticed them in the shop and recalled they were his favorite candies. She also bought him a toothbrush and a small travel tube of toothpaste along with a men's disposable razor.

"Thank you. I spoke with Sansone. She totally agreed with our decision. She even said we can stay another day if the snow hasn't let up tomorrow."

"Did you tell her about Shride?"

"Yep. She has Farrell doing some further investigating of him. They don't have enough to bring him in yet, but she thinks he's the prime suspect at this point."

"Bill, I thought of something else." She took a seat in the chair by the bed while he remained by the window facing her.

"About Shride?"

"Yes. Even though we checked with his secretary about the dates of the three murders, and we know that he could've hired someone, although frankly I can't see why, we never checked the dates of the Park Muggings."

Bill's expression changed. She had begun to take advantage of his slipping back into his old character without realizing the new one was constantly fighting for control. "Are you still at that, Courtney? Do you want to lose your job? Sansone specifically told you to stop making comparisons between the muggings and the murders."

She didn't want to push the issue, but she couldn't let it go either. "Bill, it's too much of a coincidence to me that each victim had been robbed previously around the time of the muggings." She hesitated to mention the ski mask, recalling the fiber evidence still in her purse. When she got back to the station, she had to speak with Mark about that first.

He shook his head. "Let's not talk the case right now. Let's pretend we're on a mini vacation from work. Would you like to watch some TV with me before bed?"

She found that idea appealing and was thankful his mood was back to a happier one.

They spent a few hours watching some old movies and sitcom TV shows while Bill munched on his Kit Kats, and they talked about different topics during commercials—the weather, politics, and other general issues that had nothing to do with work.

Courtney was concerned about Oliver, but she called a neighbor who had a copy of her key and asked her to go in to feed him.

When Bill's eyelids began to droop, he said, "I think it's time for bed. Do you mind helping me into it?"

Before she could reply, he said, "I'm planning to sleep in my boxers tonight, so don't worry about seeing me naked." He wheeled over to the bed and, despite his words, removed his shirt. "Just getting comfortable. I'll be too hot under all those blankets with that on."

She tried to glance away from his chest that was covered with a cropping of dark hairs. Even though he no longer worked out, his upper body was well-muscled.

She pulled away the bed covers to make it easier for him to slide in. His legs were not totally useless, but it was an effort for him to get up from the chair. She helped him into the bed, and he pulled up the covers.

"Thank you." He patted the extra pillow beside him. "Sure you don't want to join me?"

She couldn't deny the spark of attraction that had hit her when she'd seen his bare torso, but she controlled herself. "No, but thanks for the invite."

"Let's have breakfast together before we leave in the morning," he said as she hurried to the connecting door. She hoped he didn't notice her rushing to leave the room before she changed her mind.

"That sounds good." She switched off his light as she went into her own room.

# Chapter Fifteen

She also decided to sleep in her underclothes. After brushing her teeth, Courtney lay down in bed with the light on. She wished she had something to read to help her fall asleep. She was about to turn on the TV, when her cell phone rang. Ten p.m. Who was calling her at that hour? She checked the display. It was Mark.

"Courtney, what's going on?" he asked when she answered.

"What do you mean, Mark? I'm here in the City with Bill. The weather looked bad, and we decided to stay."

He drew a breath. "I know that. Sansone informed me. What I'm asking is . . . Wait, is Bill with you now?"

"No. We have separate rooms." She suddenly realized what was on his mind. "Is that what you're worried about? You've got to be kidding, Mark. I had to help him into bed." She bit her tongue after she said those words.

Mark's tone changed. "Look, I don't care what you two do. We're over, so you're free to sleep with him if you want. The reason I'm calling is that there's been a development on the case. While you two were traipsing through the snow, I had a call from Sanchez. The guy had thought over our talk and spilled."

"What?" Courtney wondered if she was sleepier than she imagined. "What did he say?"

"We were right that he was hiding something. He witnessed Hamilton's mugging last spring. That's how he knew the guy who assaulted him was wearing a ski mask."

"If he witnessed it, why didn't he stop it or call the police?" She held her phone against her ear.

"He saw the guy run away. He was more concerned if Hamilton was hurt. When Hamilton chose not to make a big deal out of it, he decided to stay mum himself. You remember Sanchez has a record. He didn't want the police to get any smart ideas about him."

She tried to absorb all of this. When she and Bill had responded to the scream of Carol White, the woman who had been killed by the Park Mugger, she had gone to her aid while Bill pursued the perpetrator. She knew how that ended, and the mugger had gotten away then, too.

"Why are you telling me this, Mark? It could've waited until tomorrow."

He paused. "I was worried about you, okay? I thought you'd want to know what was going on here. Sansone said Bill called her."

She ignored the first part of his reply and stayed on safer ground with her next comment. "What did Sansone think of your talk with Sanchez?"

"She thinks he's still holding out. She hasn't crossed him off the suspect list, even though he was at church during McCarver's murder."

"What about the ski mask? Is she still refusing to believe the killer isn't also the Park Mugger?"

"You know how stubborn she is, Court. Let's talk about this tomorrow when you're back."

"Okay. Thanks for updating me, Mark, and for your concern." She hoped she sounded sincere. The last thing she wanted was to hurt him.

"No problem." The cell phone flashed "end call," and she knew he'd hung up.

Courtney turned off the light and got between the sheets, but she knew she wouldn't sleep well. The bed, despite its size, was comfortable enough, but she had too much on her mind. She lay there thinking about the case, of Bill a few feet away, and of Mark.

When a crash sounded through the connecting door followed by Bill yelling, "Damn it!" She jumped out of bed and raced to the door.

Bill lay on the floor inches from his wheelchair. She ran to him. "Are you okay? What happened?"

He grimaced as he sat up. "I'm fine. I'll probably have black and blue on my butt tomorrow, though. I had to go to the bathroom. I didn't want to bother you. I missed my chair. Can you give me a hand up?"

"Of course." She took his hand while rolling the chair closer, so he could get back up into it. "There you go." She hadn't considered that he would need help getting into the chair if he got up at night.

"Thank you. Go back to sleep. I can manage now."

"I wasn't sleeping. It's not easy for me in an unfamiliar bed." That was at least a half truth. She didn't want to mention her call from Mark.

"I warned you that bed would be uncomfortable."

Despite her earlier insistence that they sleep apart, she found herself saying, "Maybe you're right. If you promise to leave your hands off me, I think I should stay here the rest of the night."

She thought he would be happy with her suggestion. Instead, he said, "I don't need a babysitter. Go back to your room."

"Bill, please. There's no shame in admitting you need some help."

"This doesn't happen often, Courtney. I just slipped. Now let me use the bathroom. If it makes you feel any better, I can sleep in the chair when you leave."

She wondered if he needed help in the bathroom, but she didn't dare ask. She stayed around just in case. When he returned, she was still there.

"I asked you to leave."

"I want to stay. It's only for one night, Bill. We should be able to survive that."

"What will Mark think?"

"I already told you we're not together anymore. Besides, I'm not suggesting we sleep together. Well, I am suggesting we sleep together but just in the same bed."

She thought he would still kick her out. Instead, he sighed. "Very well. What side do you want?"

\*\*\*

Courtney had to admit that Bill's bed was more comfortable. She noticed he kept as much distance as possible between them which wasn't hard to do in a King bed. He slept in the corner facing the door, away from her. She didn't fall asleep right away but kept her eyes open in the dark glancing toward the curtained windows wondering if it was still snowing. She was tempted to get up to look but didn't want to disturb Bill.

At some point, when sleep finally overtook her, she had a jumble of dreams. They weren't sinister like the previous ones or the ones she'd had for months after her mother and sister's death. These did not feature guns, fire, or blood. They were sensual. She was making love with a man, but she couldn't see his face. She felt his hands on her body caressing her nipples. She felt his hardness entering her. When she was on the verge of climax, about to call her lover's name, she woke. Daylight filtered into the room. Bill had turned and was facing her. He was still asleep. She had rolled over to him, and he had put out his arm that now hugged her in an embrace. Still drowsy, she felt as though the dream was continuing. She let her head fall onto his shoulder. He murmured, but his eyes remained closed.

She lay there watching him for a few minutes. Observing the rise and fall of his chest, the light stubble on his cheek, the lines in his face that had appeared since that fatal day last summer that changed his life.

As she watched him, his eyes flickered open lazily. She was about to turn away, when he whispered, "No, don't. Stay. Please."

When she obeyed, he moved even closer. She almost expected him to kiss her, but he didn't. He propped himself on his elbow and looked down on her smiling. "Almost like the old days, huh?"

"I knew this was a mistake."

"Was it?" He was still smiling, but something else danced in his eyes. She was both excited and afraid of what it indicated.

"I can't, Bill. I . . ."

"Shhh. I know." He placed his finger on his lips. "I'm not about to rape you. I can see the headlines now: 'Disabled Cop Rapes Partner in New York City Hotel During Snowstorm'."

She laughed, and it eased her tension momentarily. "There are enough headlines, Bill. I hope the weather's better, and we can get back to work."

His smile faded. "Do you? I think this is rather nice. The two of us together stranded by a snowstorm in a luxurious hotel, although I wouldn't mind if it was an old cabin in the woods. What matters is that you're here with me."

It suddenly made sense. She was surprised she hadn't realized it earlier. "Did you really fall out of bed, or was that your way of getting me to sleep with you?"

His words denied her accusation, but his eyes still held a hint of lust. "I did not plan that, no, but I'm glad it happened." He paused. "I need to show you something, but I promise I'll restrain myself." He suddenly took her hand and guided it toward him, lowering it to where a hard bump protruded under the covers. "Feel this. It's still attracted to you. I may have a bullet in my spine, but everything else down there works."

She thought of her aunt's words and the links to articles about having sex with handicapped men that she would be receiving from her soon. "I'm aware of that,

Bill." She tried to keep her reply flat, but her voice came out choked with desire.

"Do you want a demonstration?"

"Bill, you just said . . ."

He laughed and rolled away. "Just kidding, my dear. I'll take care of it later. Would you like room service before we leave?"

She was already sliding out of bed, eager to get away before she rushed back and did something she'd be sorry for. "I think we should get an early start if the roads permit it. We can grab something on the way."

"Whatever you want, partner. You can use the shower first, unless you want some company? Remember, I can roll right in."

"No. I'll be quick, and I'm going to use the bathroom in the other room. Let me check the weather first. Would you like me to help you into your chair?"

"I'll stay here until after you're dressed." He grabbed the remote by the side table and switched on the TV to the weather station. The snow had stopped early in the morning, but the accumulation was not as bad as earlier predictions. It looked like they could head home if they took it slow.

***

On the drive back, Bill was quiet until he dropped the bomb on her when they were less than a mile from the station.

"Court, can you tell me something?"

She jumped at the sudden sound of his voice. "Bill, you startled me. I thought you were asleep back there."

"Sorry. I was relaxing. You're a smooth driver even in the snow."

"Don't give me credit. This van's got great traction. What did you want to ask me?"

When he didn't answer, she glanced back in the rearview mirror. His eyes met hers intently. Then he looked down and drew a breath. "There's been something on my mind for a long time. Ever since that night." He paused. "You know the one I mean. Last July."

She nodded even though she wasn't sure he could see her. He needed no prompting to continue. "When I proposed to you, you didn't get a chance to answer. What would your reply have been?"

Courtney had dreaded this question for months. Myra had asked her the same one, but it was different speaking to the psychologist.

"Why do you ask this now, Bill? After all this time. What difference does it make at this point?"

"You're avoiding the question." He sounded like the cop he once was. Perhaps Sansone had been right sending him back into the field.

She took a breath. "I don't think I was ready then, Bill."

"That's still not an answer. Were you in love with me?"

They had turned the corner and were at the station. She pulled into the parking lot. "Let's not talk about this now. We have to get back to work."

Thankfully, he let the topic go, but she knew he had gotten his answer.

"I wish I had a fresh change of clothes. I think I'll go home and put some on. Sansone shouldn't mind." His words sounded flat, emotionless. She wondered if he was holding back tears.

"No, I'm sure she won't. I wish I could do the same, but I'll check in first."

"Good idea." He was already opening the door and letting the ramp down.

# Chapter Sixteen

When Courtney entered the building, Mark spotted her right away. Relief flooded his face but was replaced quickly by a darker emotion. "I see you made it through the snow. Where's your partner?"

"He went home to change. Is Sansone here?"

"In her office. Courtney, there's something you need to know. It's good Bill isn't here yet. Come with me. We can have some coffee. It'll warm you up. Even though the snow's stopped, it's still freezing out there."

She followed him into the empty break room where he poured them both a cup from the machine that was so antiquated it still took filters. She wished they'd get a Keurig machine. It would be so much easier.

"Let's go in my temporary office." He stressed the word "temporary." She followed him into what used to be Bill's office.

He closed the door and waited until she took the chair by the desk before he sat behind it. "I spoke with Sansone about what Sanchez told me on the phone, and she wants a follow up. She gave me the okay to speak with him, and she wants you to come with me."

"I thought . . ."

"Yeah, I know. She still wants Bill to work with you on the case, but she gave me the go ahead for this because we were the ones who spoke with Sanchez initially. The appointment's this afternoon at two. I was hoping you'd be back by that time. Sanchez seemed glad when I set it up. He said there are some things he wasn't able to tell me over the phone."

"Okay." She took a sip from the coffee and was glad for the warmth sliding down her throat. "I don't have a problem with that."

He raised an eyebrow. "So, how did it go with Bill at the hotel? Fancy place, the Park Lane. Did you share a bed?"

"Mark, please. I told you we had connecting rooms." She hated lying to him, but it wasn't any of his business even though nothing had happened between her and Bill.

*** 

Courtney told Mark she had to go home, change, and check on Oliver before they went to see Sanchez.

"Why don't I drop you off, and we can go straight from your place?" he suggested. Bill hadn't yet come into work, and she wondered if he was catching up on some sleep first because he seemed tired from the trip. She wondered how much sleep he'd gotten at the hotel because she'd slept more soundly than she'd expected and wouldn't have known if he was wide awake beside her.

"I guess that makes sense," she said. "If you don't mind. I've had enough driving in the last two days."

"We can take my car. I think it's better we don't use a patrol vehicle when we visit Sanchez."

She agreed. Sansone hadn't blinked an eye when they told her they were going. She hadn't even asked about Bill except to acknowledge that he would be in later that afternoon.

"What did you do?" Courtney asked when she was sitting next to Mark in his Volvo. "Don't tell me you sent her flowers, too?"

He smiled. "Nope. I think Bill's charm is wearing off on her, at least I hope so."

When they pulled up to Courtney's place, Mark said, "I'll wait in the car, but don't rush. I brought some papers along I can go over."

"You can come in, Mark. I won't take long, and it's crazy for you to wait in the car. It's freezing out here, and why run your motor?"

"Thanks." He smiled again and turned off the car.

\*\*\*

"That's strange," Courtney said as she went to unlock her door. The door slid open as she touched it. "I told my neighbor to feed the cat, but she would've locked the door behind her."

Mark put his arm on hers and slid past her. "Let me go first. Just to make sure." He switched on the light next to the door and entered. Courtney quietly followed. Oliver immediately came meowing to her, and she was relieved to see him. However, the house was in shambles. The couch was turned over, drawers and cabinets were open, their contents spilled on the floor, and several books were scattered from her bookshelf.

"Oh, shit!" she exclaimed, seeing the mess.

Mark followed her from room to room. He checked the closets and other areas where someone might be hiding, but the intruder seemed to be gone.

"I'm so sorry, Courtney."

"Who would've done this?"

"We should speak with your neighbor."

"Meaghan's a nurse. She works odd hours. I'm not sure when she'll be around."

"Did you speak with her last night?"

"Yes. I called her from the hotel. She promised to feed Oliver."

"What time was that?"

Courtney ran a hand through her hair. "I'm not sure, seven or eight. I called her on my cell. I can check the log."

Bill brought out his cell phone. "Don't touch anything. I'm going to call Sansone and report this. If you want to change and feed the cat, go ahead. Just be careful. There might be some evidence here."

"What about our appointment with Sanchez?"

"I guess that will have to wait. I'm sure Sansone will understand."

***

After the sweepers came and pronounced the place bare of evidence, Mark called Sanchez. Courtney stood listening to him but not hearing the words as she felt the violation of the ransacking cut through her.

"Are you okay?" he asked as he ended the call. "You don't look well. You should take the rest of the day off. I'll explain to Sansone."

"No. I'd rather be away from here for now. Can Sanchez see us later?"

"He said he goes to church from three to four every afternoon, but we can visit him any time after that. Are you up to it?"

"Yes. I need to get my mind off this."

"Now that everything is checked, you should go through stuff. See if anything is missing. Sansone will expect a complete report."

"I don't keep anything valuable here, Mark, but it's possible they came for the file."

"What file? Courtney, are you talking about something from this case?"

She nodded. "I know it wasn't the smartest thing to do, but I expected to bring it back after the interview with Shride. I had no idea I'd be stuck in the City. If I had, I would've brought it with me or kept it in my desk."

"Sansone is not going to be happy about it if that file is gone. Which one was it?"

"McCarver's case. It was the first one, so I wanted to see what may have initiated it. Of course, I still believe that technically it wasn't the first because no matter what Sansone and Bill insist, I think the Park Mugger is the Handicapped Strangler."

Mark didn't comment. "Why don't you go see? The sweepers are done and bagged what little they found. I doubt it's going help us find who did this."

She went to the drawer where she'd placed the file. Sure enough, it was empty except for the sweater she'd covered it with which was pushed aside.

Mark stood in the doorway watching her search. "It's gone," she confirmed. He nodded and glanced at his watch. "Sanchez will be heading to Church soon, so we have some time to kill. Have you tried your neighbor? We should talk with her."

Courtney took her cell phone from her pocket. "I guess I could see if she's around." After three rings, Meaghan answered. She sounded groggy from sleep but was awake enough to notice Courtney's upset. "Court, what's wrong? Are you back from the City?"

"Yes. Sorry if I woke you. I wasn't sure if you were home."

"I worked a twenty-hour shift yesterday. Lots of weather-related accidents coming into the ER. As soon as I got in, I fed Ollie as you asked and then went home and collapsed into bed."

That made Courtney feel guilty, but Mark was there signaling to her. "Thanks for taking care of Oliver. If you don't mind, can Mark and I drop by to speak with you for a few minutes?"

"What happened, Courtney?" She sounded alert now. "I'll go put on the coffee, and you can both come right over. Whatever it is, I hope I can help."

\*\*\*

Meaghan Mitchell lived two doors down from Courtney. A divorced woman in her mid-thirties, she'd been friends with Courtney's aunt. When Courtney moved in, she took the role of an older sister. Although they didn't get together often, Meaghan always made herself available if Courtney needed groceries picked up, her cat fed, or a delivery attended at her house. They both worked weird hours, but it often happened that at least one of them was home when the other was out.

Walking to Meaghan's house now with Mark, Courtney took a deep breath of air, hoping to relax.

"Don't worry, Court. Maybe she can help us. She probably didn't see anything, but sometimes people recall little things afterward—maybe a car parked on the street or someone odd walking around."

She nodded. She still felt guilty over keeping that file overnight.

Meaghan answered the door in her robe. Her reddish-brown curls were disheveled. At 5'9 and a few inches taller than Courtney and closer to Mark's height, she was so rail thin that she made a scarecrow look fat. Courtney, although not overweight, often had trouble keeping the pounds off. Only hours at Baxter's gym helped her remain slim.

"Come on in. Coffee's on."

Courtney smelled the aroma of the perking coffee as she and Mark entered. As directed, they took a seat on Meaghan's couch. Meaghan flitted about, getting the coffee things.

"So sorry to disturb you, Ms. Mitchell," Mark said. "But someone broke into Courtney's house last night while she was away, and we thought you might've seen or heard something when you went to feed her cat."

Meaghan stopped. "Oh, no! I'm so sorry. I wish I could help, but everything was fine when I got there. I didn't stay long. Did they take a lot of valuables?"

"Just a file, but an important one. Are you sure you didn't notice anything, maybe a car on the street near the house or someone standing around?" Mark asked.

She shook her head. "No, but I was tired and just wanted to get home to sleep. Let me serve the coffee, and I'll try to see if I can dig up any other memories."

When she returned, she sat across from them in a chair after setting out three mugs of coffee and a few Stella D'oro breakfast treats. "Sorry. I don't have much in the house. I tend to eat on the run."

*Maybe that's why she's so slender,* Courtney thought.

Taking a sip of her coffee, Meaghan said, "It was a bad night, snowing heavily when I got there. The street was full of cars, but that's because everyone was probably home riding out the storm. I didn't see anyone outside; but, like I said, I wasn't really paying attention. The warmth of my bed was beckoning, so I just put down a can of cat food for Oliver that he devoured, locked up, and left."

"You locked the door?" Courtney asked. "Are you sure?"

"Definitely. Even though I was in a rush, I wouldn't neglect that."

Mark looked at Courtney. "They checked and didn't see that anyone tampered with your lock."

"So either someone had a key or was a professional picker," she pointed out.

He nodded. "Go on, Ms. Mitchell. Do you remember anything else? Even something that seemed minor at the time?"

She looked toward Mark. "I'm sorry. I don't recall. Wait . . ." She paused. "Maybe I did see something. I didn't think much of it at the time, but there was a car parked across the street. The reason I remember it is because it was one I used to see a lot around the neighborhood and found it odd to see it there when I knew Courtney was in the City with Bill, I mean Detective Thompson."

Meaghan had always liked Bill, and she, along with Courtney's aunt, had tried to persuade Courtney to try to win him back after the shooting.

"Please explain that statement," Mark prompted.

"The car I saw was Detective Thompson's. Not the van he drives now with the hand controls, but the one he used to drive when he visited here."

Mark turned to Courtney. "Does Bill still have that car?"

"Yes, but he can't drive it, Mark. I think he gave it to Rick."

Mark turned back to Meaghan. "Are you sure it was the same car?"

"I'm not positive. Like I said, it was snowing. Most Ford Tauruses look alike. I saw it from a distance. It wasn't directly across the street."

"Was anyone behind the wheel?"

"No. It was parked. It might've belonged to one of the neighbors or a visiting relative. I work long hours. I don't know many people on the block except Courtney."

Mark glanced at his watch and said, "Thank you for your time, Ms. Mitchell, and the coffee. We should be going now. We have a meeting with a witness soon on another case."

"I don't know how you guys do it, facing crime every day."

"It can't be more difficult than facing life and death every day like you do in the hospital," Mark said.

She nodded and walked to the couch. "Take care, Courtney. If you need anything, call me on my cell. I have it on all the time, but I let it go to voicemail when I'm working. I check it for messages, though, so I'll get back to you. Don't be afraid to ask for my help. I feel terrible that someone got in your place after I fed Oliver."

She bent down and gave Courtney a kiss on the cheek.

"Don't be guilty about that," Courtney said. "You couldn't have known someone would break in. It was my fault I took the file home to begin with."

"Stop that," Mark said getting up. "No one is to blame here except whoever broke in and entered your house." He put an arm loosely around Courtney when she stood, and Meaghan smiled.

"Take care, Detective Farrel. I see my neighbor's in good hands with you."

# Chapter Seventeen

When they were in Mark's car heading toward Sanchez' place, Mark said, "If Meaghan's right and Bill's car was on the block last night, could it be possible he sent his brother to take that file?"

"That's crazy, Mark. Why would he do something like that? Bill didn't even know we'd be stranded in the City."

Mark started the car. "Who suggested you stay there?"

"Yes, but that was because the storm was worsening. Look, I'm not defending him, but I can't imagine him setting something like this up. Why would he want that file?"

"We both know he's intent on keeping Sansone from reopening the Park Mugger case. Is that why you had the file in the first place? To uncover another connection between McCarver's murder and the Park Muggings?"

"What are you suggesting?" When Mark didn't answer, Courtney realized she still had to ask him about the evidence bag containing the fiber from the ski mask that was found near McCarver's jewelry armoire when her house had been broken into just a few weeks before the first park mugging.

"I have a question for you, too, Mark. When I was clearing out our desk to make room for Bill's stuff, I came across an evidence bag. It was in your drawer."

"What?" He slammed on the breaks suddenly to avoid a bundled-up old woman crossing the street. "Damn. I didn't even see her. Why do old people walk around outside in freezing temperatures?"

"Pull over, Mark, and I'll show it to you."

He guided the car to the curb that was barely visible because of the mounds of snow that the snow removal people had dumped on the side of the street.

Courtney opened her purse and removed the bag with the fiber. She passed it to him. "It's the evidence from the McCarver break in. Part of a ski mask."

Mark's eyes widened. He took the bag in his hand. "I never took this, Courtney. Someone put it in the desk. It points to Bill, doesn't it?"

She tried to keep calm. "Mark, I know you and Bill aren't friends, and I understand why, but don't you think he'd want more than anything for the Park Mugger to be brought to justice?"

Mark handed her back the bag. "We'll need to return this. I'm not pointing a finger at Bill. I'm just saying some very strange things are going on, and he seems to be in the middle of them."

"Are you sure that's the case, Mark, or do you just want it to be that way?"

He raised an eyebrow. "Courtney, you have to admit it's odd his car was near your house when that file was stolen, and it's also strange how a piece of evidence shows up in our desk drawer right after he moves into that office."

"You're right. It's unusual, but I'm sure there's an explanation for both of those incidents. Meaghan could've been mistaken about the car, and anyone in the department could've left the evidence bag."

"Now you're reaching, Courtney. I won't argue with you because, despite what you say, you're defending Bill. Are you sure nothing happened between the two of you in New York?"

"Mark!" Her anger flared. "I won't even honor that with a reply. Now let's go speak with Sanchez. Maybe he has something to tell us that will convince you that Shride or someone else is involved in the case and stop you from trying to nail Bill or his brother just because of your jealousy."

"Very well." Mark started the engine and raced down the street. Courtney had to practically grip her seat despite the confinement of her seatbelt. Until they reached Sanchez' house, there wasn't another word spoken between them.

***

When they arrived, Sanchez' old Camaro was in the driveway. "Looks like he's back from church," Mark said. The first words he'd spoken since their argument.

Courtney noted the open door but didn't see anyone standing there or peering from the window. She followed Mark up the neatly shoveled walk. He tapped on the door. "Sanchez, we're here."

They waited a few minutes. "Is that a radio playing inside?"

Courtney heard some faint music. "Could be. Maybe he's watching TV."

"Let's check it out." Mark opened the door and held it for her calling as he walked in, "Sanchez. Are you home?"

Courtney stifled a cry as she recognized the chaos within. Like her house, the place had been turned upside down. The couch and chair cushions were scattered on the floor, the old-fashioned radio they'd heard from outside was laying on its side on the mantle, butts and glass from a broken ashtray lined the floor. Mark took out his gun and put his fingers to his lips as he inched forward quietly urging Courtney to stay behind. She withdrew her gun from its holster and followed.

As they approached the kitchen, Mark stopped. "Blood," he whispered. Courtney looked down and saw a red streak that started near the door. The lights were on in the kitchen, and Sanchez lay slumped against the refrigerator, his eyes closed, a hand across his bloody chest. Courtney couldn't tell if he was dead or alive, but Mark rushed in and felt for a pulse.

"He's alive," he whispered. "Watch your back, Courtney. I'm calling an ambulance." He took out his phone and dialed 911 and then the direct line to the department for backup.

Courtney stepped around the blood, watchful in case the shooter was still in the house. Sanchez suddenly opened his eyes. "He was here when I got home from church," he muttered.

"Did you see him?" Mark asked.

A trickle of blood fell from Sanchez' mouth, but he strained to speak. "He had on a mask."

Courtney grabbed a dish towel from the rack near the sink to help staunch the flow of blood from Sanchez' wound.

"He's gone," Sanchez said. He squeezed his eyes shut a moment, summoning his remaining strength. "He didn't get it."

"It? Is that what you wanted to speak with us about?" Mark asked.

Courtney looked down at the blood soaking through the towel and gathering on her hands. She didn't think Sanchez would make it to the hospital, but she knew Mark needed answers before the man died.

"When Joe was robbed, the guy dropped his I.D. I took it. I shoulda given it to the police, but I was still sellin dope on campus. They woulda suspected me."

"I.D., you mean student I.D.?" Mark got another rag and handed it to Courtney.

"Yeah." Sanchez' breathing was shallow now.

"Where is it?"

Sanchez put out his hand and pointed up toward the cabinet. "In a coffee can up there." He squeezed his eyes shut again. Mark got up and, without needing the step stool nearby, opened the cabinet. Courtney heard sirens above the radio.

"Say a prayer for me," Sanchez whispered as Mark removed the coffee can. "I have sinned, but God will forgive me." He closed his eyes again and lay still.

***

Mark didn't share the contents of the coffee can with Courtney until they were headed back to write up the report for Sansone. Sanchez's body was covered and taken to the police morgue where it would be examined. Courtney hoped the bullet that killed him, unlike the one that had lodged in Bill and couldn't be removed, would be identified. However, the I.D. Sanchez was hiding might be the better clue to the identity of the Handicapped Strangler who she was now convinced Sansone couldn't deny was also the Park Mugger.

"Are you going to keep me in suspense?" she asked as they drove away. Mark had pocketed the I.D.

"Hold on, Courtney." His face was grim as he pulled over a few blocks away. "I'm only sharing this with you because we're partners. Even though Sansone broke us up on this case, I still consider us a team. More than that, I still have feelings for you that I can't deny. I know this is going to hurt, and I hate to do it, but you deserve to know the truth."

"What are you saying, Mark? Whose I.D. did Sanchez leave in that can?"

He reached in his pocket and pulled out the small card. As he passed it to her, she took in a breath. She had cleaned her hands at the house, but she still felt like they were bloody. Looking down at the picture of the student, she didn't even need to read the name. The I.D. was from 2003, fourteen years ago. She was still at Baxter. Bill was a senior. "No, this can't be."

Mark took back the I.D. "I can't hide this from Sansone, but I'd like to speak with Bill first. I'd like you to help me with that."

*** 

Back at the station, they found Bill in his new office writing a report at the desk. Mark tapped on the door with Courtney behind him. Bill waved them in. Mark let Courtney enter first and then closed the door behind him.

Bill put down his pen. Although he looked across at them, his words were for Courtney. "I heard about the break in at your house. I'm sorry. I hope there wasn't much damage or that anything valuable was taken."

"It's just a mess," she said. Mark had already warned her not to mention the file. "The main thing is my cat wasn't harmed."

Bill smiled. "I'm glad Oliver's okay."

Mark walked to the desk and removed the I.D. from his pocket. He placed it in front of Bill. "Before we continue the small talk, I have some questions for you, Thompson. There was another crime committed today besides the ransacking of Courtney's place. Jose Sanchez was murdered. This is what the killer was after."

Bill glanced down at his college photo. A look of astonishment crossed his face. "My gosh. Why would Sanchez have this? I lost it on campus years ago. I replaced it, of course, but I never thought the head of security would've taken it."

"He didn't take it." Mark took back the I.D. "He found it at the scene of Joe Hamilton's mugging. It fell out of the perp's pocket."

"What are you saying? Are you accusing me of robbing Hamilton? Even if I did and, of course, I didn't, I had nothing to do with his murder. If you haven't noticed, I'm in a wheelchair and hardly capable of tackling a young, healthy man."

Mark retaliated with a different question. Courtney always admired his skill at interviewing witnesses, but she worried he was carrying this unofficial interrogation too far.

"Do you still have your old car? Does your brother drive it now?"

"My brother? What does Rick have to do with this?"

"Courtney's neighbor saw a car on the block the night her house was broken into. She identified it as the one you used to drive."

"Did she get a license plate?"

"No. It was snowing, and she was tired, but it's a coincidence the same type of car was in the neighborhood that night."

Before Bill had a chance to reply, his office door opened and Sansone stepped in. They hadn't heard her come down the hall.

"What's going on here? Lang? Farrell? Why aren't you working on the Sanchez case? I have Thompson finishing up the report on Shride. I'm still trying to build up a case to get him down here for questioning."

Courtney was glad Mark had pocketed Bill's I.D. before Sansone arrived, but she was still concerned he'd reveal the evidence they'd found to their boss. She couldn't believe Bill or Rick were responsible for any of the crimes, but there were too many odd things that connected them.

"We were just about to leave," Mark said. "I was filling Detective Thompson in on the murder." He gave Bill a quick glance and then took Courtney by the elbow. "Let's leave Detective Thompson to his report."

When they were back in their office together, Courtney asked, "When are you going to tell Sansone what you found?"

"Not yet. Thompson may be right that your neighbor couldn't accurately identify the car she thought she saw on your street; and, if Bill lost his I.D. on campus, the perp might've taken it to gain access to the school. Maybe the guy goes around stealing I.D.'s and that's how he also got in the night Hamilton was killed."

"But wouldn't he have had to change his appearance? We've already determined he was wearing a ski mask."

"He could've put the mask on later, so Hamilton couldn't identify him, and those I.D. shots aren't of the best quality. People tend to not even look at them. That's how so many underage kids get into places they shouldn't." He smiled. "I know it sounds like I'm making excuses for Bill, but you know I would be the last one to do that. Even so, I can't believe he's involved in this, but I'd like to speak with Rick privately."

"Rick never went to Baxter," Courtney said. "He got a job fixing cars right out of high school, but we both know he had a record before Bill set him straight."

"True. We need to be careful about this, Court. I can't keep this hidden from Sansone very long. In the meantime, I have a proposition for you."

"Is it one that might get me into trouble?"

"Possibly." His smile widened. "But I'll do my best to prevent that if I can. I want you at my place tonight. It's too dangerous for you to go back home right now. We can also talk more privately there and figure out how to proceed in this matter."

"Mark . . . I," she started to protest, but he waved his arm. "Don't worry. I'll sleep on the couch. You can even stop home and get Oliver and his cat supplies. I don't have any allergies to animals. As long as he doesn't wake me up at three in the morning like my mom's cat used to do, I'm fine with him staying with us."

"Okay. I guess that makes sense, but only for tonight." She had to agree she felt better knowing she didn't have to spend that night alone.

# Chapter Eighteen

At the end of the day, she couldn't help but see the angry glare Bill gave Mark as she walked out to his car with him. She wondered if he'd said anything to Sansone. She knew Mark hadn't, but she also knew he'd locked the I.D. in the bottom drawer of their desk and asked her to give him the fiber bag to put there, too. He pocketed the key. "This is just a precaution," he said. "I don't want to hand this in yet, but I'll be making a decision soon." She didn't comment. She knew he faced a tough decision.

***

Mark followed her into her house even though the door was locked. He checked all the rooms before letting her pack an overnight bag. "Coast is clear," he said. "I'll wait in the living room."

"I should tidy up before we go. The place is still a mess."

"You haven't seen my house." He grinned.

"Honestly, Mark, I hate leaving it this way."

"I understand. While you're getting your stuff, I'll do some tidying for you."

When she returned to the living room with her tote, the room was reassembled. Mark had also put back the drawers and other items in the kitchen.

"Thank you. I managed to fix the bedroom while I packed."

"Great. Now you can come back to a more normal place."

"It's not going to feel normal for me for a while." She identified with the victims of B & E's she'd interviewed over the years and wondered how McCarver felt after her house had been trashed.

Mark glanced down at her bag. "It doesn't look like you're bringing much. Most women pack the kitchen sink when they travel."

She smiled. "I pack light, and it's only for the night, remember."

He quirked a brow. "Right."

They stopped to grab a pie from a neighborhood pizza place. "I don't have much in the house, but I wasn't expecting a guest."

"I'm not exactly a guest," she said remembering the times she'd already stayed with him either at his place or hers.

"True." He bit into his slice of pepperoni pizza and then wiped his mouth of the oil and cheese. "I'm sorry your visit is under these circumstances."

They were seated at his kitchen table. He wasn't lying when he said his place wasn't much neater than hers after the ransacking. Plates and mugs sat unwashed in the sink despite the dishwasher. The stove was covered with bags of snacks, some half open with bag clips closing them. There were bits of food and other debris on the tile.

"I think I need to return the favor and help you clean up here," she said drinking from one of the bottles of water he'd placed on the table for them. He knew she didn't like beer which was the only other beverage in his fridge. Sodas were toxic, and he'd never developed a taste for wine.

"I won't stop you, but it may take some time. You haven't seen the rest of the place."

She smiled. "I'm aware of your attempt to keep me here longer, Mr. Farrell."

"You always were good at reading people. The place isn't any worse than when you used to stay here." He took another bite of pizza and a sip of water. His eyes seemed to warm as they looked at her. Although the kitchen featured fluorescent lighting, it looked as if a candle had flickered over his face.

"It's hard to recall." She almost bit her tongue. She hadn't meant to be insensitive.

He didn't seem to notice. "Why do you think we stayed at your place so much?"

"Mark, let's not dwell on the past right now. I'm thankful for your offer for me to stay here, but it's only for one night as we agreed. If you want, I can repay you by doing some housekeeping, but that's where my gratitude ends."

He nodded. "I understand. Don't worry. You owe me nothing. I'm just doing a friend a favor."

***

Mark insisted on sleeping on the couch. He told her he'd changed the bed that morning and assured her that his bedroom was one place that hadn't been hit by the "Farrell bomb," as he termed his messiness. Courtney still had a hard time falling to sleep on the double bed. It was comfortable enough, but her thoughts kept her awake. She knew Mark planned to reveal the evidence they'd found to Sansone the next day. He told her he had no choice. What Sansone would do when she found out was another matter. It was possible Bill had lost the I.D. and that the person who had robbed Hamilton had found it and used it for entry into the campus. The other alternative seemed unlikely. Why would Bill steal money from a deaf co-ed? Even more implausible, if the person who mugged Hamilton was the same one who strangled him and also the Park Mugger of dozens of victims last summer, how could Bill be connected? He had been shot and crippled by that same perp.

When Courtney finally fell asleep early in the morning, she should've expected some nightmares, perhaps even a repeat of the one she'd had earlier. Instead, this dream took the form of one she'd been battling since before she became a cop ten years ago. It was a sunny, warm day in August. She'd been arguing with her mother and sister before leaving the house. There was her mom, arms crossed against her ample chest, "Where are you going so fast, young lady? I asked you and Lisa to clean your rooms and take that cigarette out of your mouth. What did I tell you about smoking inside?"

"But Mom." She crossed her chest in the copycat way she often used to mimic control of Francine Lang and took another drag of her Marlboro. "I'm meeting a few friends. We're going to the beach." She was in her final year at college in the fall and old enough to leave the house without her mother's permission.

"She's really meeting Devin," Lisa said. She stood by her mother's side. Courtney and Lisa were four years apart but not close sisters. They had their own interests and groups of friends. Lisa enjoyed nothing more than getting Courtney in trouble with their mother who always sided with her youngest, saying that Courtney took after her bum of a dad who had left when the girls were babies.

"What if I am?" Courtney asked. "I'll clean my room later. You treat me like a child, Mother. I'm twenty-one, for Pete's sake."

"Go on then. Meet your boyfriend, but you'd better have your room spotless when you return." Her mother's face was red. She was on blood pressure medicine, and that was a warning sign her numbers were up. Courtney slammed the door behind her, ignoring her mother's angry face and her sister's sly smile.

The scene erupted into red against the dark sky. Fire enveloped Courtney's home—flames devouring it in its angry mouth. Firetrucks lined the driveway. Neighbors looked on shaking their heads and whispering. She ran around them, but a fireman grabbed her.

"My house! That's my house! Where's my mother? Where's my sister?"

The fireman's face darkened. "We have a man inside. You have to stay back, ma'am."

Dark smoke billowed from the chimney. A fireman came out the front door wearing a mask. He pulled it off and took a large gulp of air. He spoke to the fireman who had restrained her. "They're gone, Joe. The smoke got them before the fire. We'll remove the bodies after this is all cleaned up. We have to stop it from spreading."

"No!" Courtney cried, remembering a cigarette butt she'd carelessly tossed on the floor near some papers in her room, her angry words to her mother and sister. She tried to run forward again, but another fireman pulled her back. He, too, wore a mask but it wasn't the same one the man who'd pronounced her family dead had worn. It was a black ski mask. She pushed away from him, but he held her tight. She grabbed the mask and tore it off. Sanchez stared back at her and then took a cigarette from his pocket, lit it, and tossed it at her. Her clothes went up in flames. She screamed in horror, rolled on the ground to douse the flames, but their red tips only grew higher. She wondered why the firemen weren't coming to her aid. All she could see was red. The heat of the flames was unbearable. She kept rolling and screaming until something stopped her. Someone had come to help. She felt his hands around her. The flames started to recede.

"It's okay, honey." She felt strong arms embrace her. "Courtney, wake up. You're just having a bad dream."

She opened her eyes to see Mark holding her against his naked chest. The bed covers were tossed on the ground. For a moment she forgot she was at his house. She forgot they were no longer lovers. She fell against his chest crying. "Oh, God. I thought I was being burned alive."

He smoothed back her hair, stroking it gently. "You're still having those nightmares. You really should go back to Myra and speak with her again."

"This one was different," she choked. "In the others, my aunt arrived as she did that day and took me home. In this one, I was put on fire by Sanchez. He wore a mask like the Park Mugger, but I saw his face when he took it off."

"Court, that's just your subconscious reliving the trauma and your experience finding Sanchez' body." He tipped her face up and gazed into her wet eyes. His lips moved closer to hers, but he stopped before they met. He let her go and glanced down at himself. Besides being shirtless, he only had on his boxer shorts, and a large bump indicated he was aroused. "Sorry. I should've put some clothes on. I heard you screaming. I ran in as fast as I could." His face reddened. Courtney was only wearing a thin nightgown herself, and her upturned nipples were clear through the see-through fabric." She pulled the sheet back over her.

"What a mess I made of your bed."

He grinned, and it lightened the sexual tension. "Don't worry. I toss and turn a lot myself. Lucky you didn't fall off the bed."

He moved away an inch, but Courtney felt it was a gulf. "Don't go." She whispered the words. "I'd feel better if you stayed. Please."

He considered a moment and then slipped into bed next to her. She laid her head on his shoulder. "I'm not going anywhere, Court. Try to get some sleep. It's very early."

But she was wide awake. "Mark, do you believe nothing happened between me and Bill in the City?"

His lashes hooded his eyes as he replied. "Why are you asking that?"

"Because there's something I've never told anyone, but I want to tell you."

"Courtney, it's okay. I know you still have feelings for him."

"Please, Mark. Let me finish." She took a breath. "Before Bill was shot last summer, he proposed to me."

He looked down. "Did you accept? Obviously, he took back his offer when he realized he would condemn you to a life of caring for an invalid."

"No, Mark. That's not it. I hadn't given him an answer. Myra told me that if I'd really loved him, I would've fought to get him back no matter how incompetent he felt. But the truth is, if he hadn't been shot that night, I would've answered him, no."

Mark looked back at her, a stunned expression on his face. "Is that true? I always thought . . ."

"You thought he stood between you and me, but you're wrong. I have feelings for him, but they're more friendship than love, and maybe now they're mixed with a bit of pity. It's different with you."

"What are you saying?"

"Sleep me with me, Mark. I want to be with you again."

Just as he embraced her, a cry from the hall startled them. It was Oliver standing in the doorway.

Mark laughed. "Not now, kitty. Your owner has something more important to do than feed you."

# Chapter Nineteen

After they'd made love, Mark must've felt some vibes coming off Courtney because, as he held her in his arms, he said, "Court, you have to stop feeling guilty over everything. The fire that claimed your family was a tragic accident. What happened to Bill wasn't your fault either."

"I wish I felt as convinced of that as you do, Mark. They determined the cause of my family's fire as a cigarette butt. I haven't touched a cigarette since then. As for Bill, I was with him that night. We were partners. I was supposed to back him up."

Mark glanced down at her, his eyes full of sympathy and love. "He told you to help the vic. You were only following his orders."

"But she was already dead, Mark. There was nothing anyone could've done for her. I should've been his backup." Tears sprang to her eyes. She wiped them away with the top of the sheet that she'd pulled up over her.

"You have no way of knowing that if you'd gone with him to pursue the mugger that you wouldn't have been shot, too. Court, you might've been killed. And, about your house fire, was it definite the stub was the one you smoked? You said you left in the morning, but the fire happened late at night. That seems an awful long time for a butt to flame."

She rolled away from him. "You're just making excuses for me, Mark, and I appreciate your trying to help, but I'd rather not talk about this anymore. We should get up. We have to get to work."

Mark sighed, touched her back. "I wish we could stay here in bed all day, Courtney. This morning was wonderful. But you're right. We have to get back to the real world. I need to share the evidence we found with Sansone. I'm not looking forward to that. It doesn't make sense that Sanchez had Bill's school I.D. or that his car was near your house when that file was taken. I hate to say it, but I still think Rick's involved."

Courtney was sitting up, pulling her nightgown back on. "We'll see what Sansone thinks."

Mark chuckled. "You know she's a bit biased toward Bill and his brother."

"She's a cop, Mark, a good one. She won't let her personal feelings get in the way of evidence."

"In a way, I wish she would. You know how I feel about Bill, but I can't believe he or his brother are killers." He got off on his side of the bed. "How about a shower together before we head to the station?"

She smiled. "Only a quick one."

***

It turned out not to be so quick, as the shower turned into another lovemaking session. When they finally got dressed, and Courtney fed Oliver, it was almost ten o'clock. They were officially an hour late. Courtney was surprised Sansone wasn't calling her on her cell. She was usually at the office by eight every day.

When they arrived, Courtney discovered why no calls had been made. Sansone rushed out of her office, signaling them. She looked more upset than their lateness warranted.

"It's about time you two showed up," she said. It was obvious she realized they'd spent the night together. "Thompson's out sick today. I need you"—she looked at Mark— "to help me question Shride. His driver just called and said they were on their way."

"Wait a minute," Mark said. They hadn't even had coffee before leaving his house and Sansone had cornered them before they could grab a cup from the station's pot. "There are some things we need to talk about first."

"No time," Sansone said. "Meet me in the interview room."

"What about me?" Courtney asked. "What do you want me to do?" She was surprised that, since she had gone to Shride's office in Manhattan, Sansone would choose Mark to interview the lawyer instead of her.

"I'd like you to go to Bill's place and get some of the files on this case that he asked to bring home last night. I need them for the interview. He also has Shride's file. I need that, too."

"Did you ask him about them when he called in sick?" Courtney found it odd that, after Mark had shown Bill the I.D. and told him about the car her neighbor identified, he would not come to work the next day.

"I didn't. His brother was the one who called. You can call him if you'd like. I don't have time." With that, she took Mark's elbow and pulled him toward the meeting room. At that exact moment, Shride burst through the door. His face was red as he stomped toward them. "Your receptionist is very rude. She asked for I.D. as if she didn't know I was scheduled to see you. I have a meeting at noon, so this better be quick."

Sansone released Mark. "I understand your time is valuable, Mr. Shride. This shouldn't take long. Please come this way." A phony smile was plastered on her face. Courtney wondered why this man who was way ruder than the department's secretary was being treated so politely. She watched as Shride followed Sansone down the hall to the meeting room. Mark, a few paces behind, looked back at her and winked.

***

Something felt wrong to Courtney. She called Bill's cell from her car, but it went directly to voicemail. Maybe he was sleeping. She had his home number but, when she called that, the same thing happened. Sansone said Rick had called Bill in sick. Did he go out and leave his sick brother home in bed? He could've gone to the drugstore to get some medicine, or maybe they were at the doctor's office. She decided just to go there and find out for herself.

As she drove through Baxter's white streets, she noticed the snow had started again. The forecast hadn't called for it, and it seemed light, only a few flakes tapping her windshield from time to time. While part of her mind was on what she would find at Bill's house, she also couldn't help thinking about what had happened between her and Mark. Had her defenses been dropped from that terrible nightmare? Was she ready to commit to him, to anyone? He hadn't proposed and then gone on to be shot but neither had they argued and his home gone up in smoke. He was right. She couldn't kick the guilt of how her mother and sister died and how Bill had become crippled.

A horn blaring behind her caused her to quit philosophizing and realize she was stopped at a green light. She murmured an apology to the unknown driver behind her and continued on her way. People could be impatient even on icy roads.

When she got to Bill's house, the curtains were drawn. Both cars were in the driveway--Bill's van and Rick's Taurus, the one Meaghan had thought she'd seen on the night of Courtney's break in.

The path up to the door was unshoveled. She wondered why Rick hadn't cleared it. It would be slippery for Bill's wheelchair. She rang the bell and waited. When no one came to the door after she'd tried a few times, she was about to turn around and leave, when Rick answered.

"Courtney. What are you doing here?"

"I heard Bill was out sick. I hope he's feeling better. Captain Sansone asked me to come pick up some files he brought home last night."

A puzzled expression drew across Rick's face. He shook his head. "I'm sorry. I have no idea where he may have put those, and he's resting now."

"What's wrong?" Courtney asked. Despite Bill's disability, he was rarely sick.

"Not sure. It might be a flu." He began to close the door.

"Wait. If you let me in, I may be able to locate the files. I won't disturb him, I promise." Courtney knew Sansone would not accept her returning empty handed.

Rick paused. "Okay. If you insist. Come in."

When Courtney entered the house, she got that strange feeling again that something was wrong. Mark termed it "detective's intuition" or as Bill said, "relying on the gut." It was what often made the difference between life and death for a cop.

But Rick was smiling as if things were fine. The smile, however, was a bit too wide. "Bill's downstairs resting. I'm afraid he fell asleep looking at the files. I'll go get them for you. Have a seat in the living room. I won't be long."

Courtney wanted to ask how Bill managed to get down to the basement, but she knew Rick had installed several apparatuses for his disabled brother and imagined there was an elevator or some sort of lift to transport him.

While she waited, Courtney couldn't shake that weird feeling. After what seemed like a long time, Rick called up to her. "Courtney. Can you come down here, please? Sorry, but I'm having a bit of trouble finding the files."

Courtney had never seen the basement before. When she opened the door that led from the kitchen, she noted the ramp that had replaced stairs. The lights were off, but when she touched the switch by the door, they didn't turn on. She descended into darkness.

"Rick," she called. "I can't see. Where are you?" She didn't want to speak too loud in case Bill was still asleep, although he may have awakened when Rick had called to her.

She landed safely at the bottom of the ramp and looked around. The basement seemed to be composed of more than one room. Likely, it took up the length of the house. The one in which she arrived was full of storage boxes, their dark bulk filling the space. The wood-panelled, walnut walls made the area seem smaller. A door led to another room. It was closed.

Smelling a faint odor of dampness, common to old houses and underground rooms, she felt spooked. Why hadn't Rick answered? She checked for the gun at her side and then realized she'd forgotten to put it on this morning in her rush to get to the station. This was crazy. Bill and Rick were friends. They couldn't mean her harm.

"Courtney," Rick's voice came from behind the closed door. "We're in here. Let me get the door for you."

She took a step back involuntarily as the knob moved, and Rick stood in the doorway. The lights behind him were also off, and she couldn't make out where Bill was.

"What's going on with the lights?" she asked. "Why is it so dark down here?"

"Sorry. I have a call in to the electrician. We've been having problems since yesterday. Only in this part of the house." He opened the door wider, and Courtney finally saw Bill. He was slouched in his wheelchair, still sleeping.

Rick put a finger to his lips and tiptoed a pace back, which Courtney also found odd because he'd called her from down here without waking his brother.

She followed him into the room. That's when she saw them. The pile of files lying on the floor in front of Bill. At first, she thought he'd dropped them there as he fell asleep but then she saw the kerosene cans next to them.

Rick suddenly grabbed her. A gun was placed at her head. "Don't move. I didn't want to involve you, Courtney. You're a rather nice lady for a cop." He moved his hands over her body, frisking her. "No gun? That makes it easier." He released her, throwing her toward Bill's chair. She nearly rammed into it, but caught herself before she fell.

"What's going on, Rick? What are you doing?"

"No time for explanations."

He took a lighter from his pocket. "Stand back. I know you don't like fire much and this is going to be a biggie." He grabbed a can of the gasoline and spread it atop the files. Courtney gasped, icy fear runnning up her spine. She looked at Bill. He was still asleep, but hardly breathing. "You've drugged him, haven't you?"

Rick smiled that eerie smile again. "You were always quick, Court." He stepped forward with the lighter. "As soon as I set these files on fire, I'm getting out of here. Don't try to escape. There are no windows down here, and I'm locking the top door. I hope it'll be quick and painless for both your sakes."

"Oh, my God! Rick, please. Just tell me why you're doing this?" Then she realized the horrible truth. "You were the one with Bill's I.D. You're the one who shot him. You're the Park Mugger."

"Like I said, no time for explanations." He lit the papers, and ran.

Courtney stood there frozen as the flames leaped up, burning the files to cinders, arching up the wood walls. Smoke filled her lungs. She began to cough. Bill slept on in his drugged slumber. If she didn't do something fast, they would both be dead.

# Chapter Twenty

In a moment of panic, there are a lot of things that race through one's mind. Courtney recalled the day she came home to find her home on fire, her mother and sister trapped inside. There she was, watching the flames envelope the ranch house, the acrid smell of smoke burning her throat. A fireman was telling her to stand back.

"Let me through, please! That's my house! I need to find my mother and sister! Are they out?" She glanced around desperately.

The fireman continued to block her way. "We're doing what we can, ma'am. You need to stay where you are."

As dark smoke continued to billow from the chimney and red sparks flared like fireworks, erupting in bursts of flame, a fireman wearing a mask came out the front door. He threw it off and took a large gulp of air. "They're gone, Joe. The smoke got them before the fire. We'll get the bodies out after this is all cleaned up. We have to contain it first." He glanced toward the onlooking neighbors.

"No!" Courtney screamed, pulling away from the fireman who restrained her.

Suddenly, Aunt Violet was there. "Come with me, Sweetie. We can't do anything."

"No!" Courtney yelled again. "Let me go. I have to save them. There must be something I can do." While she struggled, tears falling from her eyes, the flashback receded, and she became aware of the present. She and Bill were stuck in this inferno with no means of escape. As the flames edged toward them, she knew the whole room would soon be engulfed and then the fire would spread up through the rest of the house. She had to act quickly to save them. This time she wouldn't fail. Ramming herself against the door was useless. It just hurt her shoulder. In circumstances like this, she thought she'd be endowed with the super human strength those in life threatening situations often gained, such as mothers lifting cars off their babies and people crawling out from under tons of a collapsed building's debris. But it didn't seem to be happening to her. She cried in frustration and gave the door one last bang. Although the frame protested, it didn't give way. However, the loudness of her attack caused Bill to stir.

"Courtney," he said groggily. "What are you doing here?" Then he remembered. "Oh, my God, no! Rick." He choked on the smoke that was inching closer to his chair. She'd moved him as far out of the way as she could up toward her and the door.

"He's gone. There's no time to talk," she cried. "The door is locked. I can't budge it."

"Maybe I can." She watched as he maneuvered his chair so that the back was facing the door and slammed into it. At first, nothing happened. But when he repeated the attempt, the door finally gave. She rushed out behind him as smoke billowed in their trail.

"Help me up the ramp," he instructed as he turned the chair around. She pushed him up, panting from a scratchy throat as fire engines and police sirens blared in the distance. At the top of the stairs, they found Rufus tethered by his leash to a kitchen table leg. The dog panted as Courtney unwrapped his leash. "Don't worry, boy," she murmured. "You're safe with us."

As they emerged from the house, inhaling fresh cold air, Courtney saw Mark pull up and race out of his car. "Courtney, are you okay?" He hugged her as Bill looked on. For once, he didn't seem angered at Mark's show of affection toward his old girlfriend. Rufus even licked Mark's hand when he went to take his leash from Courtney.

\*\*\*

They put an APB out for Rick and found his car abandoned a few miles away. The search then spread to the airport. In the meantime, Bill was questioned at the station by Courtney and Mark. He sat with his head in his hands, the horror of what his brother had done finally hitting him. Rufus sat nearby, whining softly.

"I should've known," Bill said. "Rick was always in trouble as a kid. I tried to protect him. My father was an alcoholic and couldn't keep a job. My mother worked around the clock to put food on our table. When she finally kicked him out, the damage had already been done. Rick idolized him. He never took up drinking, but neither did he want to work for a living. He spent a few years in juvie. You have his record. I thought he had finally straightened himself. After I was shot, he did so much for me. I didn't realize it was because of the money I gave him. Why he killed those people I can't imagine." He covered his face again.

"He was also the one who shot you," Courtney said gently. "He confessed to that while you were asleep. It may have been an accident. He was fleeing from the scene in the park. He had his mask on, so you weren't able to see him, and it was dark."

"My God, all this time. They have to find him. I want to know why."

Mark took over the questioning at that point. Courtney just felt like she was tearing a band aid from a wound way too slowly.

Sansone was in a tizzy. The news was already spreading like wildfire online and in social media. A police officer's brother had set fire to his home and escaped. Indications pointed to his being both the Park Mugger and the Handicapped Strangler. Rick's photo was flashed across the media along with Bill's. The phones kept ringing, and reporters swarmed outside the station.

In all the insanity, Shride had been released. He stormed out threatening a lawsuit for insufficient evidence. Things didn't calm down until around three p.m. Mark took advantage in the brief lull to take Courtney aside. He motioned her into his new office. "Something's not right. It's hard for me to believe Bill knew nothing about what was going on with his brother. Also, he has no idea where Rick would be hiding out. The airport search turned up empty. Since we found his car, he either stole another or is on foot. He wouldn't be stupid enough to take public transportation with his photo all over the place."

"I know there are a lot of things that don't make sense," Courtney acknowledged.

"Damn right. Rick's being the Park Mugger is hard enough to swallow, but it fits because he has a history of theft. But why change his m.o. and start strangling previous victims?" Mark got up and turned to face the case's suspect board that was identical to the one in Sansone's office. Rick's photo was now displayed in the spot Shride's had occupied. The three victims were arranged on the opposite side. "There must be something that connects those three besides the earlier robberies and their disabilities."

"Maybe that's why Rick burned the files," Courtney theorized.

"Yes, but how did he know Bill would bring them home? And why would he attempt to murder his own brother?"

"We're back to the fact that Bill insists he knows nothing," Courtney said. "Do you want another round at him?"

"No. Sansone is speaking with him now. She's trying to be delicate. I mean if he's telling the truth, the man just found out his brother is a killer, and his house is severely damaged by fire."

"I think we'll know everything once they catch Rick."

The phone on Mark's desk suddenly rang, jarring the silence. "I guess the vultures are starting up again." He turned away from the crime board and picked up the receiver. "Farrell here."

Courtney watched his face change as he listened to the caller on the other side. "What? Knowles? Let me transfer you to the captain. Hold on, please."

Courtney waited while Mark sent the call through. After he hung up the phone, he said, "That was Shride's office. His secretary called to inform us that while her boss was here being questioned, Knowles stole two mil from the company account and disappeared with the money."

"Shride's partner?" Courtney recalled the man she had met when she and Bill had gone into the law office in the City. "What do you think this means?"

Mark seemed to be weighing this new information in his head. "The only conclusion I can draw is that Knowles is connected with this case somehow. He may have been working with Rick and could be with him now. We need to find out their connection. I'm sure Sansone will ask us to do that."

# Chapter Twenty-One

As Mark predicted, Sansone was eager to get to the bottom of the situation. She called Bill into her office with them.

"I'm sorry to keep questioning you, Bill. I know Farrell and Lang did a thorough job, but some information has come to light that might explain what was behind your brother's actions."

The use of Bill's first name wasn't lost on Courtney. He was still Sansone's pet.

Bill had wheeled into the room, head lowered, Rufus beside him. Courtney had no idea where Bill and the dog would stay now that their home was fire damaged. She also could tell he was still in shocked disbelief about Rick.

At Sansone's words, he raised his head and looked at them gathered around her desk. "There's been news?"

Sansone tapped the top of her closed pen on her desk. Courtney noted the flowers were gone. "Yes. I'm afraid not good news. Bill, did your brother know a man named Jonathan Knowles?"

"Shride's partner? Why would he . . . . Wait," A light of awareness lit up behind his eyes. "I didn't connect it when Courtney . . . . Detective Lang and I met him. I mean the last name is common enough, but . . . Oh, my God, that was years ago. It can't be Brenda."

"Who's Brenda?" Mark asked before Sansone could.

"Brenda Knowles was Jonathan's younger sister and Rick's girlfriend. He was pretty serious about her. That was back in the days when he was a streetsmart kid committing petty robbery. She had a minor record, too. I think they were part of a gang of some type. Rick didn't share much with me about who he hung out with. I never met Jonathan, but I guess he knew him."

"You said 'was'," Courtney said. "Where is Brenda now?"

"She's dead. I don't know the details except that she was shot, but I think it happened during something they were involved in. Rick came home one night, his shirt soaked with her blood, and told me he was through with the life. I guess that's when he learned a tough lesson, but somehow it didn't stick."

"Could Rick have killed her?" Sansone asked.

Bill shook his head. "No. I'm certain of that. I may not have known my brother well, but he loved Brenda Knowles."

"It could be that Jonathan believed Rick was responsible for his sister's death," Mark interjected.

"I wish that were true, but it looks like they were in this together—for the money. Any luck finding them?"

Sansone tapped her desk again. "Knowles is a rich man. He has the money to buy protection."

"We still don't know why they chose those victims and who was behind everything."

"We won't know that until we catch them." Sansone's eyes held a glint like a predator on the loose. "It won't be easy, but we're going to do that. I have a plan."

As her voice dipped, Bill rolled himself forward while Courtney and Mark leaned toward Sansone to hear what she had in mind. Even Rufus took a few steps forward, his paws clicking on the office tiles.

"First we have to speak with Shride again. I think he'll be more amenable to talking to us now that his company is bankrupt. Then we track down any of Knowles' contacts, other family members, anyone who can shed some light on what happened to his sister." She glanced toward Bill. "Thompson, you run a check in the library for any reports of the death of Brenda Knowles, obituary, case files, anything you can find."

He nodded. The use of his last name made the command stronger.

"Farrell and Lang, I want you around when I get Shride back here. I also want you both to follow up with any of Knowles' acquaintances. I've already ascertained that he's never been married. There's a possibility he's gay but still in the closet, despite today's relaxed attitude. He might have a boyfriend somewhere that can lead us to something." She tapped some keys on her computer. "Here we go. One of the tabloids ran a rumor that he was involved with Fred Brody."

"Brody?" Isn't he that actor in the soap opera? What's it called?" Mark scratched his head.

"*The Tamed and the Wild*," Sansone said with a slight grin that Courtney wasn't used to seeing. "Although he has an apartment in Manhattan, he also has a place not far from Baxter. I'd check it out first." She jotted the address down on a pad, tore off the page, and slid it across the desk. Mark took it. "On it, Captain."

Bill echoed his response. "I'll be off to the library archives for that info you want, too. Do you mind if Rufus tags along? I still have to make arrangements for a place for us to stay."

Sansone, approving of both her male detectives' plans, nodded. "Very well. We're going to crack this before the media hangs us."

*** 

When they were in Mark's car heading to the address Sansone had given them for Fred Brody, Courtney asked, "I don't understand something. How can we investigate out of our jurisdiction? Wouldn't the local P.D. need to do that?"

Mark took his eyes off the road for a second and gestured toward his visor where he'd placed the warrant to search Brody's home. "Sansone has her way of getting around formalities. Besides, the crimes all took place in Baxter so, with the permission of the other precincts, we pretty much can oversee things."

Courtney still didn't totally understand, but she was glad to be away from the station. The weather had warmed, and the snow was melting. The van splashed through the slush.

"Do you think he's there? Brody?"

"I suspect not," Mark said. They were a block away from the place, according to his phone's GPS. They had used his personal car instead of a squad car. Sansone had suggested that in case Brody was in occupancy. "We might still find something. If he's out, the warrant gives us access."

Courtney wondered why Knowles had two homes. She imagined the one only a few miles outside of Baxter was where he met with Brody for their trysts. It would be safer, if less comfortable, than his penthouse in the City.

"Two rich men," she said. "Shride and Knowles."

"Yes, and now Knowles is richer."

"But how was he involved in the muggings and murders?"

"That's what we need to find out."

\*\*\*

Courtney was shocked when they pulled up to the small ranch on Maple Street. Out front was a prominent realtor's sign claiming the property was for sale.

"Can we still search it?"

"Of course. C'mon."

They expected not to find anyone home, but Mark rang the bell, anyway. It was answered promptly by a short man with a crop of hair that was obviously a toupee.

Courtney was not a fan of soap operas, but she wondered how Fred Brody could be such a draw for his viewers. In sweatpants and displaying a stubble of beard, he looked like a slightly overweight, middle-aged man.

"Can I help you?" he asked. "Are you here about the house?"

"No," Mark said. "Are you Fred Brody?"

"That's me. What is this about?"

Mark flashed his badge. "I'm Detective Farrell from the Baxter P.D. and this is Detective Lang. We're here to speak to you about Jonathan Knowles."

The smile left his face. "I have nothing to say about him. I haven't seen him in six months."

"We have a warrant to search this house."

"Wait a minute. There's nothing here you'd be interested in. I'm only staying until the place gets sold and then I'm heading back to New York to shoot more episodes of the soap."

Mark persisted, nudging himself in the space Brody had left when he took a step back. "Then this won't take long."

Brody stepped back further and allowed them to enter. "Go ahead. You won't find anything."

"Tell us about Knowles," Courtney said as she followed Mark inside. "Are you aware he's absconded with the money from the law firm he partnered with Harrison Shride?"

"What?" Brody looked genuinely surprised. "That's crazy. I know he hated Shride, but I would never expect him to steal from the guy. He had enough money of his own."

Mark was walking around the room, surveying it. Courtney remained talking with Brody. "Why did he hate Shride? They seemed to get along well enough when I visited there with Detective Thompson a few days ago."

Brody kept his eyes on Mark but answered Courtney. "That was an act. Jon could've been an actor like me if he hadn't chosen law, but I guess putting on a show is one of the requirements for being a lawyer. Maybe that's what attracted me to him."

"Can we sit down?" Courtney eyed the couch.

"Sure." Brody waited until she sat on the sofa and then joined her. "I can't really offer you anything. The place is pretty empty. There's a few beers in the fridge, though, if you can drink on the job."

"No. I can't." She was amazed at how relaxed he was as Mark searched his place. Either he was as good an actor as his soap character or he was telling the truth about Knowles.

"How long did you two, uh, know one another?"

"Two years. We met when I hired him to look over one of my contracts. He wasn't a contract lawyer, but I'd heard good things about him."

"You were referred?"

"Yes, by one of my co-workers."

"We can get the name of that person later. Explain why you think Knowles hated his partner."

Mark had returned from finishing the search and said, "The place is clean. No sign of Knowles or anything suspicious."

"Of course not," Brody said. "I told you we split six months ago. He left the place to me. It was the least he could do, but I'm heading back to the City soon. I have no reason to stay here now."

"Please answer Detective Lang's question. Why did Knowles hate Shride?"

"Wouldn't you if he'd killed your sister?" Brody said it as if it was common knowledge.

# Chapter Twenty-Two

Mark took a seat next to Courtney, recognizing that this new information would take some time to process. "Tell us how it happened," he said.

Brody shrugged. "I don't know all the details, man. He told me they used to hang together—the four of them as teens—Jon, Shride, Thompson, and Brenda. Rick Thompson was in love with her, but I think Shride had a thing for her, too."

"Then why would he kill her?" Courtney asked. Even more puzzling to her was why Knowles would then go into business with Shride.

"It was an accident. Shride was the only one who carried a gun. He stole it from his adoptive father who kept it in the house for protection. Jon told me this in confidence. He was kind of drunk when he did, so I'm not sure the story is totally accurate." He folded his fingers into a temple and glanced toward them. "Thompson was always the one who got caught. Shride was better at getting away. He was the older one and also the leader. I think he picked up tricks from his father. Jon said that night they had broken into a gas station. It was late, and the guy was about to close up. Shride sent Rick in. He was always the patsy. But when the attendant pulled a gun on him, Rick backed away. They all wore masks, so they couldn't be identified. Shride took out his gun and aimed it at the man, thinking he would hand over the money. Instead, he called the cops on his cell. Shride thought he had no choice but to kill him before they arrived. Brenda begged him to leave it be. Rick started to run away. Shride always called him 'the chicken.'"

He took a breath. "They'd never killed anyone before, but Shride needed the money. He had to pay off a debt. It was for coke. They all experimented with drugs back then. He drew his gun, but Brenda jumped in the way. When she went down, Rick picked her up and carried her. I don't know how he managed to run holding her, but she was a slight thing, and he was pumped up with adrenaline. They managed to escape to an abandoned house they sometimes used to stash their goods, party, and plan their next heists. When they brought Brenda in, she was unconscious but alive. Rick begged Shride to take her to the hospital, but Shride said they couldn't do that. There would be too many questions. The attendant hadn't seen their faces, but he knew one of them had been shot. Jon agreed with Thompson. He didn't want to see Brenda die. He convinced Shride to call a doctor he knew who would keep things quiet. But when the man arrived, Brenda was already gone. Shride paid the doctor to dispose of the body. Brenda had run away from home at sixteen to her older brother's house. Other than Jon, she had no family. Their parents were abusive drug users that neither of them kept in touch with."

"So they never caught them," Courtney said. It was a statement, not a question.

"No. But Thompson quit after that. He was heartbroken. He went to his brother, Bill, and promised to turn over a new leaf. Bill welcomed him with open arms. He knew there'd been trouble. He saw the blood on his shirt that night and knew about Brenda, but he promised to protect Rick if anyone asked questions. That never happened."

"So Bill knew all about this?"

Brody nodded. "Yes."

"So how did it come about that Shride and Knowles became lawyers?" Mark found this part of the story hard to believe.

"After Thompson left, Shride and Knowles parted ways. They split the money they had. Thompson hadn't wanted any of it. He called it blood money, and said he could always rely on his brother so wouldn't need it. He regretted that decision later because, unlike Jon and Harrison, he couldn't kick his drug habit. It's ironic that Jon and Shride ended up going back to school to study law. They were both smart men. Once they cleared the drugs out of their system, they had no trouble earning their degrees. Shride's dad, a lawyer, was particularly proud of him. They graduated the same year and met up a few years later at a professional association dinner. That's when they decided to form their law practice."

"Obviously, Knowles still held a grudge against Shride about his sister's death."

"I would say. He talked about it bitterly but not often. I think he was trying to avoid the memory. When he spoke of Brenda, he said she'd been an angel, the only one who truly understood him and that he'd failed his obligation as an older brother to protect her. I got the impression he wanted to find a way to make that right." Brody kept his eyes on Mark. "Of course, Thompson had never forgotten her. He had even more of a motive to avenge her death."

Mark looked over at Courtney and then back at Brody. "We have a lot more questions, but I think we need to do this at the station. Will you come with us?"

Brody glanced at his watch. "Oh, man. I have the realtor coming in a half hour. They're showing the place today."

"You don't need to be here to do that." Mark's voice tightened, "and I was being nice about the invitation. You don't have a choice, Mr. Brody. Now come along, or I'll have to handcuff you."

Brody shrugged. "In that case, sure. Lead the way, Detective."

# Chapter Twenty-Three

Sansone was pleasantly surprised they'd brought her a witness, but she had done some legwork herself. "Bring him to the interrogation room. I'll question him with you, Farrell. Thompson's still working on getting Shride down here, and I want you," she looked at Courtney, "to speak with Myra while we're occupied. I've scheduled Thompson with her after you."

Courtney didn't understand. She imagined the case took priority and not a session with the staff psychologist, but before she could complain, Sansone gave her that glare that meant the conversation was over. She stood up and beckoned Mark and Brody to follow her down the hall. Courtney had no choice but to head to Myra's office.

Myra was waiting for her. "Come in, Courtney. Have a seat."

Now that she had obeyed her captain, Courtney felt free to question why she had to speak with the psychologist. "Why does Sansone want me to talk with you, Myra?"

Myra waited until Courtney sat in the chair next to her desk. She avoided the shrink couch because she didn't expect to be there long.

"You were trapped in a flaming house and have had no time to process the fact you almost died. I know your history. I requested this talk. How are you feeling?"

Courtney didn't like the scruitinizing gaze Myra sent her. "How am I supposed to feel? I want them to find Rick and Knowles and make them pay. My priority is the case, not talking to a shrink."

Myra laughed. "Good. You're angry. That's part of the healing. Now tell me, how did you feel when you learned Rick was behind this? What do you feel about Bill now? And Mark?"

Courtney didn't like discussing her feelings. She thought some things needed to remain private. "I was shocked about Rick, of course. I can imagine how Bill feels. It's his brother, for God's sake."

"Yes, I'll be speaking with him next. But right now, I want to know your feelings. Has the experience changed your feelings toward Bill and Mark? Have you overcome the guilt from your family's fire?"

"Don't do this, Myra. Please." Courtney stood up. "I don't want to discuss the fire or my personal feelings toward Detective Thompson or Detective Farrell. But, if you must know, I'm back with Mark. I feel sorry for Bill, but I never loved him. If he hadn't let me go after he was shot, I only would've stayed with him out of pity. I realize that now."

"That's a breakthrough. I need to see how he feels about that, though. He's lost a lot—his brother, you, his ability to walk."

"He's a survivor, Myra. He'll get through it. I'll help. He's still my co-worker and my friend."

Myra nodded. "Yes, he'll need your help, Courtney. And you're a survivor, too. Don't forget that."

***

Courtney was still absorbing Myra's words when she realized Bill was outside the office. She stood up to leave.

"No, stay a minute," Myra instructed. She went to the door and opened it.

"Sorry, Sansone said I should see you. I thought you were free."

"That's okay, Bill. I'm done talking with Courtney, but I actually would like to speak to both of you together if you don't mind."

He rolled himself up to her desk opposite Courtney. "That's fine. I guess." Courtney could tell he was hesitant.

"Where's Rufus?" she asked.

"Sansone's got him in her office. I never took her for a dog person, but she even gave him part of the hamburger she had an officer pick her up for lunch."

Courtney smiled. It was a relief to talk about something not as serious as the things Myra had brought up.

The psychiatrist went back behind her desk. "I'm glad the dog is doing well, but I have to ask you both a few things." She looked from one to the other ending on Bill. "First, I want to ask you, Bill. How are you feeling?"

"How do you expect me to feel? I just found out my brother killed three people and crippled me. How would you feel, Doctor?"

Myra drew in a breath, but Courtney knew she must've expected that answer. "I would be angry and hurt, and I'd want to do something about it."

"Exactly, so why am I wasting time talking to you?"

"Examining one's feelings isn't wasting time, Bill. You need to work through this. Tell me what you'd like to happen when they find your brother and Mr. Knowles."

"I don't understand. Are you asking if I want to see them go to jail for their actions? Of course I do."

"That's not what I'm asking. I want to know what you personally want done to them. How would you want them to pay for what they did to you?"

"That's a loaded question." He glanced at Courtney. She didn't understand why Myra had wanted her to stay.

"Exactly," she mirrored his words. "So what's your answer?"

He took a breath and looked back at Myra. "There's no way they can pay for what they've done to me. I trusted Rick. I thought he'd grown up, changed his ways. When I was shot, he took me in, made accommodations to his home—all on my money, of course. But I don't understand." His voice quivered. He fought to keep it under control. "The only explanation is that Knowles brainwashed him. Rick was never very strong emotionally. It wouldn't be hard for a more dominant personality to control him." His words hardened. "You asked what type of revenge I'm seeking. I'd like Knowles dead. I'd like to kill him." His hands balled into fists. "I don't know about Rick. I wouldn't be able to forgive him. I'd just like him to explain."

"And what about Courtney?" Myra changed the subject abruptly. "How do you feel about the fact that she's made up her mind finally and chosen Mark over you?"

He avoided Courtney's gaze as he replied. "I think I knew she never loved me even the night I asked her to marry me, the night that changed my life. That's why I insisted we break up. Because if she stayed with me, it would only be out of pity. Then, stupidly, I convinced myself I may have been wrong. I thought it was Mark who clouded her judgment, that if I hadn't been so hardheaded and sent her away, we would've had a chance."

"How do you feel about that now, Bill?"

He turned his chair to face Courtney. "Now I know, and I wish them well. Everything in my life has changed, but I can still make a difference. I still have a reason to live. Call it vengeance, call it justice. I want to find my brother and Knowles and have them pay for what they did to those victims and me."

# Chapter Twenty-Four

After they left Myra's office, Mark and Sansone had finished speaking with Brody. Sansone was in her office writing up the report. Rufus lay sleeping in a sunny spot by the window. Bill nodded to Mark and went back to his desk. He said he had to continue his research on Knowles. Courtney got the impression he wanted to leave her alone with Mark.

"Everything okay?" he asked as they stood in the hall together.

She looked up into his eyes and saw concern there. "Yes. Myra just wanted to make sure Bill and I were coping with any emotional issues from our experience at his house."

She could tell Mark knew she was skirting around the fact that the "experience" as she called it, was a fire, the one thing she had feared most of her adult life. "Let's go back to the office. I'll get us some coffee. This is going to be a long day."

"Was Brody released?" She waited while he stopped at the department coffee machine and brewed two cups.

"Yes, but he can't go anywhere. His house sale will have to wait." He grinned wryly.

Back in the office, Mark sat behind the desk while she took the chair opposite it. "I hope your talk with Myra did some good for you and Bill. I assume you didn't just talk about the fire."

She knew one of the reasons Mark was so good at his job were his developed powers of observation. "No. She helped us put things in perspective. She knows we're back together, and Bill approves. He accepts it."

"I'm glad." Mark smiled wryly again. "God, Court, I almost lost you. It's just starting to hit me. We have to catch them." His hands became fists, and Courtney recognized the same need for vengeance and justice that Bill had displayed in Myra's office.

"I think we're all in agreement on that. Are there any leads yet? Did Brody reveal anything we can use?"

"Nada. Sansone thinks he's telling the truth that Knowles cut him off months ago."

"So what's our next move?"

"Shride is coming back. He's not happy, but now he realizes we're on his side."

*** 

While waiting for Shride to return, Courtney felt like she needed a break. She decided to head to the gym and then to the firing range to work off some of her tension. She sweated out a grueling round on the treadmill and exercise bikes, spiking the speed and times of her usual workouts. Sweat dripped off her face as she ran a circuit around the track and then bench pressed fifty-pound weights.

As she headed to the locker room to shower and change, Officer Lisa Mullins called out to her. She and Lisa had trained together when Courtney first joined the Baxter P.D. Lisa now worked in narcotics.

"What's doing, Court? I saw how you hammered yourself. Is something wrong?" The short-haired blonde wiped a hand over her brow. A few strands of hair fell free from her red bandana.

"Hi, Lisa. I'm fine. I just needed a good workout today. I've been missing sessions at the gym."

"Looks like you made up for it. Are you sure you're not working off some sexual frustration?" She smiled. "Last thing I heard you and Mark were having some issues."

Courtney felt a bit embarrassed that rumors about her relationship had spread through the department. "No. We're fine. We had a small falling out, but we're back together."

Lisa nodded, but she didn't move. Courtney imagined she was blocking her way to the locker room to get more information.

"I see. From my own experience, I can tell you that once you break up with a man, things are never the same again."

"We didn't actually break up, Lisa. There were some misunderstandings." *Why did she feel she had to explain herself?*

"I guess they involved Bill. I don't blame you for moving on. He's a nice guy, and it's a shame what happened to him, but you want a man who can take care of you, not the other way around."

Whatever anger Courtney had burned off with exercise, returned. "I don't need any man to take care of me, Lisa. Now if you don't mind, I need to change. Please move."

"Sure thing. I didn't mean any offense." She raised her arms and stepped away. "Have a good day, Courtney. Hope you got all your frustrations out."

Courtney ignored the remark and cleaned up quickly. She was still simmering when she got to the firing range. She noted there were few officers there and was happy for the chance to have some peace to practice her shooting. After a few rounds of hitting the target nearly dead center, she felt better. As she was about to head back to her office, she was surprised to hear the squeak of wheels. Turning, she saw Bill arrive with his gun. He rolled up next to her.

"Hi, Courtney. I see you've been practicing, and it looks like you've nailed your target well." He looked toward the poster of a man that now contained an array of bullet holes in its chest.

"It helped that I was mad. I ran into Officer Mullins in the gym, and she said some things that upset me."

"Mullins." Bill put a finger to his head as if he was trying to recall who she meant. "Ah, yes. The blonde gossip who hasn't been able to move up the ranks since she started here. She's been jealous of you for ages, Courtney."

That made her feel a little better. "Well, I guess I should be going. I've had enough for today."

"No, wait. Don't you want to watch me? I could use a cheerleader."

She smiled, but she realized he needed the support. He probably hadn't been at the range since before his accident.

"Are you able to, you know . . ."

He grinned. "Yes. I can fire a gun. Look." He raised his weapon, aimed it high and shot straight at the target, hitting it through the heart. He continued to pull the trigger until all the bullets were emptied. Courtney was amazed that his aim was perfect, even from the lower angle.

"You certainly haven't gotten rusty," she said.

He turned back to her. "Nope. It was easy. I just had to pretend that guy up there was Knowles."

# Chapter Twenty-Five

Shride returned. He appeared pale and looked as though he'd aged in a matter of hours.

"I don't believe this," he said when he was seated in Sansone's office with Courtney, Mark, and Bill. "You think you know someone for years. You trust them, and then they do something like this." He waved his fleshy hand.

"I can relate," Bill said. Courtney knew he was thinking of his brother.

"You realize that we can't try you or Mr. Knowles for crimes you both committed as teenagers, Mr. Shride," Sansone said, "but your partner is guilty of more than stealing from you. We have reason to believe he was an accomplice with Mr. Thompson's brother in the muggings of multiple people and the killing of three disabled individuals."

Shride bowed his head. "I was afraid of that. Knowles was always manipulative. I thought it was a good trait at first. He was the one who brought in our clients. He convinced people I was in charge, but he was always the leader, even back when we were running the streets."

Sansone tapped her pen against her pad, and Rufus' ears perked up, but the dog remained quiet. "Do you have any idea where he'd go? He's still in the country, and we're consulting with the FBI to find him and Thompson, but we need your help. Money tends to talk and is very easy to hide behind, but having known him so long, despite being blind to his revenge scheme, you might have some thoughts you can share with us."

It was a surprise to Courtney that the FBI was now involved, but it made sense. The press was closing in. The manhunt for the Park Mugger, the Handicapped Strangler, and his co-hort were featured on social media. Rick and Knowles' photos were splashed across the paper on Sansone's desk.

Shride raised his head and ran a hand through his white hair. "Actually, I do." He leaned forward. "I can tell you exactly where they are, and that's why I'm here."

# Chapter Twenty-Six

"When we first started looking for a space for the law firm, Knowles suggested we check out a place in Westchester. He never liked the City," Shride confided. "There was a building with an office available. We had a big argument over it when I insisted we headquarter in Manhattan."

"So what makes you think he and Thompson are hiding out there?" Sansone asked.

Shride ruffled his hair again, uprooting several white strands. "It's just a hunch, but I know you need to follow all leads. Also, he mentioned it awhile back. He said the building was up for sale again, and would I consider a move? I wondered why he'd kept up with it."

"How long ago was that?" Sansone was jotting on her pad.

"I'm not sure. A couple of months maybe."

Courtney could see the wheels spinning in the captain's head. "Do you have an address for us?"

Shride reached into his pocket and pulled out a card. "I don't know why I kept this, but I brought it along today." He handed it to Sansone.

She glanced at it and said, "Thank you, Mr. Shride. We'll look into this." She turned to Bill. "Detective Thompson, can you please do a check on this property?"

Bill came over to her and took the card she extended. Courtney caught a glance of a real estate logo but couldn't make out the address. She wondered why Sansone was still including Bill on this investigation, but she knew he needed to be involved. She also realized that Sansone was bypassing the FBI, something that might cause her grief and possibly the loss of her job. It wasn't the first time the captain had taken such an action. During the investigation of the Park Mugger last year, there had been a clue that Courtney hadn't followed up on. She'd gotten hell from Sansone about it at the time because a special agent had taken the credit for it, although it ended up being a dead end. The point was that it clarified for Courtney that Sansone was a competitive policewoman. She wanted to be the one to catch the people behind these crimes and put her name back in good standing in the headlines.

They waited while Bill went to his office to check on his computer. He returned quicker than they expected with a grim turn to his lips. "That property isn't in Knowles' name," he stated. That fact was clear because they'd already run a check on all of Knowles' holdings.

"So who does it belong to now?"

Bill took a deep breath and looked around the room. "It's in the name of Rick Thompson. It's my brother's building."

# Chapter Twenty-Seven

Mark questioned Sansone's decision to send him and Courtney to the address of Rick's building. "I thought the FBI was in charge of this now," he said.

Courtney caught the slight upturn of Sansone's lips when she replied, "They may not know about the building yet. I'll inform them once you check it out. Don't worry. You'll both have plenty of backup."

"Captain, I'd like to request to go, too," Bill said. "If Rick is with Knowles, I want to be there."

Sansone hesitated. "I'm not sure that's wise, Detective Thompson, but I can understand why you'd want to be part of this. You can accompany them, but only with the backup officers. I don't want you going in. That would be way too dangerous for someone in your condition." Her eyes focused on his wheelchair.

Courtney thought he would argue with her, but he nodded. "That's fine. I just want to be around if they catch them."

\*\*\*

Courtney and Mark suited up with bulletproof vests and comms units. As Courtney got into the unmarked car Sansone suggested they use, she couldn't help but feel they might be going on a wild goose chase. Even if the building belonged to Rick, there was no guarantee he and Knowles were hiding out there. That might explain why Sansone wasn't giving away the tip to the feds, but she knew the bigger reason was that their captain hoped the two fugitives would be there and that her department would receive the credit for their arrests.

\*\*\*

"I have a bad feeling about this," Mark said as they entered the building. Their weapons were concealed because they didn't want to alert the other tenants. Shride had told them that the office Knowles had been interested in was on the top floor which happened to be the third.

They took the elevator up. "They may not even be here," Courtney said, trying to convince herself it was safe. Sansone had theorized that if they were in the building, it was a temporary hiding place until they could secure fake I.D.'s and things died down enough for them to leave the country. Bill had been of the opinion that they already had the I.D.'s and they wouldn't wait too long to get away. "You'd be surprised how much money can buy," he'd said. "If they're still around, there must be some unfinished business they have."

The top floor was a wide space with only one office. With doctors and dentists on the bottom two floors, Courtney could understand how Knowles would've valued it as a law office. Mark placed his finger to his lips as he moved quietly toward the door. Courtney followed his actions, tiptoeing in her flats. When they were close enough, she could see a nameplate on the wood. Krueger and Findlay, Esq. Were those Rick and Knowles' new aliases, or a dummy front?

Sansone's voice came through Mark's mic, making them both jump. "We've got you in view and can hear everything. Take it slow." Then Bill's voice came through Courtney's. "If Rick is there, I'm coming in." She could hear the buzzing of Sansone's argument about that, but Mark already had his hand turning the office knob. His other was locked on the gun at his side. They walked into the dark space, taking opposite sides of the room. Silent shadows seemed to fill the space along with stacked boxes. Courtney wondered what was in them and considered they might be the reason the two men had returned here, but were they still around?

Mark was canvassing the left side of the room. There was an inside door. A light shone under it. "Courtney," he whispered, "over here." She followed him, placing her own hand around the bulge at her hip.

Mark opened the door, and there they were, smiling at them. Rick held a round object in his hand. Knowles had his arms across his chest. "Welcome, detectives. I assume Shride ratted on us. No harm done. We were just about to vacate this office, and Thompson had the great idea to demolish this building on the way out. You see, Shride was right. This wasn't a very lucrative location."

"What are you talking about?" Mark demanded. He'd drawn his gun and was pointing it at them. Courtney was momentarily distracted by Sansone's voice telling her that Bill was headed into the building. She said they'd just received an anonymous tip that an explosive was on the premises, and they were calling in the bomb squad.

"I'd put that away if I were you," Rick told Mark. "I didn't want to use this until we were out of here, but it's quite sensitive and the timer is already ticking away."

"Mark, it's a bomb," Courtney whispered.

Mark edged slowly forward but lowered his gun. "There are innocent people in this building. If you disconnect that bomb, we'll give you a head start out of here."

Knowles laughed. "Who are you kidding? I know you've got men outside. As far as killing innocent people, none of them are innocent. They're all going to die eventually. Like McCarver, Hamilton, and Fredericks."

"Why did you kill them?" Courtney resorted to stalling them. The bomb squad would arrive quickly.

Knowles laughed again. "I didn't kill them. Thompson did. Tell them your story, Rick."

Rick's hands seemed to be slightly shaky around the bomb, and Courtney's heart raced with fear that he might drop it. She knew Knowles was the mastermind behind everything and had used Rick for all the dirty work.

Before Rick could reply, Courtney heard the elevator doors open. For a moment, she hoped the bomb crew had arrived, but she knew they would've taken the stairs. She turned to see Bill rolling into the room.

"Welcome, brother," Rick said. "I heard you escaped the fire, but I think an explosion should do the trick to take you out of your crippled misery."

"Bill, stay back," Mark said. "He has a bomb."

"I don't care what he has," Bill said, his face reddening. "Why are you doing this, Rick? Why did you try to kill me and Courtney?"

"I was just about to tell them."

"Make it snappy, Rick," Knowles said. "We don't have all day here. Time is ticking away, you might say."

Courtney knew Knowles was eager to get out of there and that he didn't plan on taking them along. Even if she and Mark and the people downstairs escaped, it would be much harder for Bill to make it out of the building. She wondered why Sansone had allowed him to join the team when it was obvious he would do something stupid like try to help. There was only silence now from the other end of their connection, and Courtney only hoped it was because the bomb squad and FBI were on their way and their rescue was out of Sansone's hands.

"This won't take long, Jon." Rick glanced toward Bill. "Did you really think I'd gone straight after Brenda's death, brother? I needed the coke even more then. I couldn't just ask you for money for drugs, could I? The muggings helped support my habit. If you recall, I wasn't working then. It was just an accident that you and Courtney got in my way that night in the park. I couldn't let you catch me, but I didn't mean to seriously injure you. Oh, well, sometimes things happen for a reason."

Courtney watched as Bill's face grew redder as he listened to Rick's story. She hoped he'd find a way to keep him talking; but, like Sansone, he was keeping quiet. It was Mark who asked, "So what started the murders of those disabled people? If you were still using, why didn't you steal from them, too?"

"Everyone thought I was being a good brother taking Bill in after he became crippled. What choice did I have? It was the least I could do since I caused the injury. Besides, I used his money to start a business. It was a front, of course. Many of my dealers were website clients. Bill was too busy feeling sorry for himself to notice."

"I don't understand," Courtney said, "How does Knowles fit into all of this? And you still haven't explained why you started killing people."

Knowles sighed. "For Pete's sake, hurry the story along, Rick. It's the last one they're going to hear, but it doesn't have to be a novel."

Courtney wondered how much time was left on the bomb.

"Okay. Let me cut to the chase. Jon and I reunited right before I shot Bill last year. He found me through a fellow acquaintance." He smiled. "You might say a fellow cocaine dealer. Anyway, we both acknowledged that we never justified Brenda's death. Jon wanted to take Shride down, and he offered me a split of the money if he could do it. I would never have to rob anyone again. His plan was simple. He wanted to frame Shride for murder. After all, Shride had murdered Brenda in both our eyes. I was the one who suggested we kill handicapped people. Easier to disarm them and, what do they really have to live for? Also, by then I was pretty sick of Bill—helping him out of bed, taking him to the bathroom, being his nurse." He looked toward his brother. "I have to admit you've made a lot of strides towards independence since then."

Courtney watched Bill sit there wordlessly but with a calm as ready to ignite as the bomb in his brother's hands.

Knowles picked up the story. "It was a brilliant idea. Your little brother is actually quite smart despite the fact you always considered him the black sheep of the family." He addressed his words to Bill now. "I was aware of Shride's history. I had the files on previous disabled clients. I knew Rick could pay you a visit at work and plant some evidence, and then I made that anonymous call to you about Harrison. I asked Rick to destroy the files on the victims as a precaution to cover our trails, but it was his idea to off you as an added bonus. It would've worked well except your old girlfriend"—he glared at Courtney— "had to get in the way before we finished our work." He stepped forward and, before she knew what was happening, Courtney was in his grasp with a gun against her head.

Mark started to lunge forward, but Rick extended the bomb. "Don't move, or I'll toss this."

Courtney knew there were people like the 911 assassins who would give up their lives for a cause. She hadn't thought Rick and Knowles would be in that category, and she was even more surprised she'd been grabbed, but they had to make their way out of the building somehow.

"C'mon," Knowles said, "We're getting out of here." He began to drag Courtney along as Rick followed, holding the bomb out.

When they were in the hall, Knowles said, "We all take the elevator. Our ride is waiting outside. Only this lady comes with us. The rest of you stay. If you're lucky, the bomb people will get here in time to disarm the device. If not, oh, well."

He pressed the button, and Courtney watched in fear as the elevator doors opened. She heard Bill murmur to

Mark, "I'm so sorry. This is all my fault. If anything happens to her . . ." He didn't complete the sentence, but Courtney knew the two of them were trying to figure out a plan to free her.

She was surprised the elevator was heading up and not down. She expected Rick and Knowles to make their getaway in a car. Instead, when they arrived at the roof, a helicopter was waiting for them.

Knowles pushed her inside as Rick continued to hold the bomb out as he backed into the helicopter. A black man she didn't recognize sat at the controls. She assumed he was hired by Knowles.

As the helicopter rose, she could see the line of police cars below and wondered why they weren't shooting the copter down. Then she realized Sansone had probably learned she was being held as their hostage and had held back the fire.

Courtney's last sight of Mark and Bill were as they raced to the edge of the roof as Rick tossed down the bomb. She closed her eyes in anticipation of the explosion that would kill more innocent people—the man she loved, and her best friend.

# Chapter Twenty-Eight

When Courtney opened her eyes, they were high above the building, but it was still in one piece. She turned to her captors. "Looks like your bomb was defective. Lucky for you, you won't have additional murder charges."

Knowles dug the gun deeper into her back. "Shut up. I know how to put together a bomb or get someone to do it for me. That was a decoy. Your idiot cop friends couldn't tell the difference."

"By the way, I don't think I've introduced you to Bruce." He looked toward the helicopter pilot. "He's just dropping us off on our midway point. We have a lot of traveling to do."

Courtney was relieved Bill and Mark were safe, but she wondered what Knowles was planning. "Why did you take me?" she asked.

Knowles laughed. "To assure our escape, of course. Your life is worth a lot, Detective. I'm sure your boyfriends will be scouring the country for you, but I have a special hideout even more secluded than the office. We stay there until things calm down a bit, and then off we go. At least, off Rick and I go."

She didn't have to ask what would happen to her. Although he'd confiscated her gun and comm unit, he hadn't found her cell phone that was hidden in her bra.

"How do you intend to leave the country when your faces are all over the press and social media?" she asked instead.

"That's really none of your business, but we have some disguises, and we aren't stupid enough to use the airport."

"I guess you have a private plane somewhere, too."

"Nope. We're taking the train to Canada. Railway to the Rockies."

Now she knew she was going to be sacrificed. They couldn't keep her around after telling her their plans. She looked over at Rick. Maybe there was a way she could appeal to him. He was the weaker of the two psychologically, but she had a feeling he was high on drugs. Up close in the cramped interior of the copter, she could see the signs on his face, the redness of his eyes.

As if reading her mind, Knowles said, "You're pretty quiet, Rick. Don't you want to speak to your brother's girlfriend and let her know what we have in mind for her?"

Rick remained expressionless and said dully, "I don't care what you do with her, Jon. I just want to get outta here."

"I'm surprised." Knowles replaced the gun at her back with his hand and gently rubbed up and down. It felt worse than the metal. "Don't you want to have some fun with her before we dispose of her? Get a taste of what Bill the Cripple, sampled?"

Knowing Knowles was gay made his hands on her even creepier. She said a silent prayer that she would be rescued before either of her captors made good on Knowles' suggestion.

\*\*\*

When they were at an altitude where the building below them looked like a model from a toy construction set and Mark and Bill were mere dots on the roof, Rick blindfolded her. "No use you seeing where we're going even if you wouldn't be able to tell where it is," he said. She felt his breath on her neck.

The helicopter took a few turns, but she couldn't tell in what direction they were headed. When they landed after what seemed like hours, Rick undid her seatbelt. Knowles was talking with the pilot. She heard the flap of a wallet opening and the sound of bills changing hands. She imagined Bruce was being well paid for the flight.

"Get up," Rick ordered. "I'm removing the blindfold now because the footing up to our hideaway is a bit steep."

"Good idea," Knowles said. "We wouldn't want her falling and breaking anything before she's done helping us." That followed by a loud guffaw.

The area in which the copter set down was surrounded by rocks. No houses seemed to be located nearby. Courtney saw that they had landed on a ledge. Rick pushed her out of the copter and Knowles shadowed her on the other side as Bruce took back to the air.

"Now we head up to the cabin," Knowles said. "Watch your footing. It's quite a climb."

She took a minute to look around. They were on a rugged mountainside of trees and rough boulders. She looked up to where Knowles pointed and saw a cabin some five-hundred yards beyond, up a steep trail.

Courtney was in good shape due to regular excerise at the department gym, but she was out of breath by the time they'd scaled the pathway. The cabin, more of a small house, fully appeared as they crested the top.

"There's no cell reception out here," Knowles told her. "So if you were thinking about using your cell phone to call for help or send some GPS coordinates, that won't work. We're going to confiscate it, anyway, just in case. But let's get you inside where it's cozier."

Her heart beat at the words that were far from innocent. Whereever they were, she feared that Sansone and the FBI wouldn't be able to reach them.

\*\*\*

Knowles took a keyring from his pocket and opened the rusty door. Rick nudged her inside. The place smelled of rot. As Knowles switched on the lights, she saw the half-eaten bags of junk foods that littered the floor—pretzels and potato chips, some squashed into the tiles. Clothes were scattered about, and a computer was set up on a table with three legs. As Rick brushed by it, he tapped a few keys, and she could see the outside of the cabin and the side of the mountain.

"Please excuse the mess. We left in a rush. The bedroom is neater."

Courtney stepped over a can of Pringles as Rick, at her side, pushed her forward with the butt of his gun. She flinched at the thought there was only one room in which to sleep, not that she would get any.

The room into which they walked featured two bunk beds and a cot in the corner. "Rick likes it on top," Knowles grinned. "I guess that pertains to women, too. You can take the guest bed." He indicated the cot which looked like it belonged in an army barracks. She imagined the mattress was as hard as a rock.

"Unfortunately, we don't have any clothes for you," Knowles continued. Rick's had a few women here, but they always took their stuff back with them."

"She might fit into my pants," Rick said, "although they might be a bit large." He opened a drawer and threw a few pairs on the cot along with some striped shirts. "There's also a shower, although the water runs cold most of the time. It's better than an outhouse, but no windows for the steam or anything else to escape."

"Good one, Rick." Knowles guffawed again. "Why don't you make yourself comfortable, Courtney? I'm going to check the security cam, not that anyone would be stupid enough to come after you out here. We'll be taking turns throughout the night watching the mountain. There's some scraps in the fridge if you get hungry. Rick is a good cook. Bruce will bring some provisions in a few days along with our rail tickets. We won't be here very long."

Courtney knew that once they boarded the train to Canada, they would have no need for her. She prayed Sansone was working with the FBI now to locate her.

"One last thing," Knowles added, "Rick is also very good with computers. He created a very interesting setup here. If anyone is spotted on the cam, automatic rifles that are built into the house's foundation will fire at the target. It's quite effective at keeping people away. Rick activated it as soon as we were in."

He walked to the door. "I'll be back later. Rick, why don't you help Courtney relax a little?" He smiled as he left the room. Courtney stepped back as Rick approached.

"What's the matter, honey? Afraid of your old lover's baby brother?"

Courtney knocked into the edge of the cot behind her and nearly fell onto the bed.

Rick grinned. "I may have been mistaken. Perhaps you're actually eager for me." He touched the zipper of his pants.

Courtney couldn't help but notice his large hands. For the first time, she realized they were disappropriate in proportion to his body. She imagined them wrapped around the necks of Agnes, Gloria, and Joe, choking the life out of them.

"Don't touch me," she warned. "You're nothing like your brother. You've never grown up. You're still a drug addict, and now you're a murderer."

The smile remained on his face, but she could tell it had lost its shine. He moved his hand away from his fly. "Okay, bitch, I'll leave you alone . . . for now. But I promise you, when Jon gives me the word, I'll show you how much more of a man I am than Bill. That'll be the last taste of pleasure you'll ever know."

Courtney knew he planned to rape and then strangle her as soon as their cohort was back with the train tickets and they'd made it safely to the Canadian Express. She shivered both from the cold in the unheated cabin and his words. She said a silent prayer that Sansone and the FBI were tracking her. But even if they managed to find her despite the lack of wifi connection to her cell phone, they would be gunned down as soon as they approached the cabin. Her only hope was retrieving her gun and overpowering Rick and Knowles. She had been trained in karate so might be able to unarm Rick, but Knowles was the one she worried about. He was stronger and smarter than Bill's brother and would be much more of a challenge.

# Chapter Twenty-Nine

She was thankful the two men left her alone. She could hear them talking in the next room.

"That bitch is playing hard to get. I'll show her. Bill never had the guts to put her in her place, but I'll be happy to do that."

"Take it easy, Rick. We have more important things to worry about. Bruce hasn't gotten back to me. He was supposed to call after he picked up the tickets."

Courtney wondered if Bruce had absconded with whatever money they'd given him for the helicopter ride and taken the train away himself. If that's what had happened, Rick or Knowles would have to leave the cabin. That would give her a chance to make her move with the odds being more in her favor.

"I sent him several texts, but he hasn't replied," Knowles continued. "I knew we shouldn't have paid him anything until we had the tickets. I'll give him until tomorrow morning. If he doesn't respond, you're going to have to take the jeep and finish the job."

Courtney had hoped Knowles would be the one who would go.

"Isn't that too risky?" Rick protested. "They have our photos everywhere."

"I've got a disguise for you. I'll help you apply it. In the meantime, leave Ms. Lang alone."

"You really are a party pooper, Jon. If I have to risk my life out there, I want to at least have a little fun first."

"We'll see. Let's just wait until tomorrow. I might allow you to say a sweet goodbye to her."

They both laughed at that. Despite the shiver that ran up her spine, Courtney focused on the fact that

Knowles had a functioning cell phone. How was that possible? She checked her cell but saw it was dead. She was surprised they hadn't asked for it yet. Even though she had no way of charging it, she searched for a place to hide it and placed it under the cot's mattress.

Rick and Knowles were still talking. "So what's for dinner, man? I think we should celebrate tonight. At least Bruce followed instructions and packed the fridge."

Rick replied, "I'm not in the mood for a big dinner, but I can whip up something."

"Wonderful! In the meantime, I'm going to spend some time with Courtney. I should fill her in on the rules around here just in case she's getting antsy. I wouldn't want to bore our new guest."

She backed away from the door as Knowles' footsteps approached.

"Hello, Ms. Lang," he said as he entered the room and took a seat on the cot. "I see you're making yourself comfortable here. I'm glad." He faked a smile. She refused to look at him.

He pretended not to notice. "We've run into a slight snag. Our pal Bruce seems to have stood us up. I'm giving him a few more hours. If he doesn't show, Rick is going to take care of things. That may delay our departure a bit, but I promise you we'll be out of here soon."

She knew their plans didn't include her except for use as a hostage in case they were identified. She had to figure a way to get a message to Sansone.

"You said there's no cell service up here, so how can Bruce get in touch with you?"

He leaned against the bunk beds and regarded her like an entymologist studying a bug. "You're a smart lady, Courtney, but you'd be even smarter if you didn't ask questions. I actually can't answer that. Rick is the tech guy here. He's rigged a private line for our use. So far, there's been no communication which leads me to believe Bruce either skipped or has been caught. I don't like either scenario, so I'm preparing Plan B."

"Why wait then? Wouldn't it be wiser to act now?" Even though Rick would be the one to go, she would at least even the odds if she could get one of them out of the cabin. With night coming, it might also afford her an opportunity to disarm Knowles if he fell asleep.

She saw Knowles considering her suggestion. "You do have a point. Darkness would be a better cover for Rick, too. Thank you, dear. I'll go tell him I've moved up our plans."

After Knowles left, she heard him conferring with Rick. "You what?" Rick said. "She's just trying to get me out of here. Don't you see that?"

"What she says makes sense. We need to act fast. Now let me set you up with the disguise. Remember, you go to the depot, purchase the tickets, and then get back here asap. If you have any problems, let me know immediately. Without the jeep, I'm pretty much stranded here, but I have to take that chance."

"I still think you're making a mistake, Jon. If you're sending me out, I want some of that payback you promised before I go."

Knowles laughed. "You'll have your money when I have the tickets. Now get your ass in the bathroom, so I can work on your face."

"What if I refuse?"

"Then we may both end up behind bars. There's a good chance they got Bruce."

"But they can't reach us here. It's safer in the cabin with the protection around the base."

"Yes, but we can't stay here forever. Bruce didn't stock the refrigerator for more than a few days. We need to get out of the country."

There was a short moment of silence and then Rick said, "Okay, but if you won't give me my part of the settlement, I want that go at Courtney that you promised before I leave."

"Fair enough, but don't kill her … yet."

\*\*\*

As Courtney heard Rick's heavy footsteps approach, she had to think fast. Despite Rick's technical know-how, it was obvious Knowles was the brain of the duo. She devised a plan to trick Rick and get his gun.

He closed the door behind him as he entered, a glint in his eye. "We don't want Jon listening in on our personal activities, do we?" he said as he slowly approached. "You have no idea, Courtney, how I've dreamed of this moment. All the times I saw you with Bill. When you two broke up, I wanted badly to jump in and take his place, but you hooked up with that Farrell guy. Now you'll see what you missed."

Instead of the struggle he expected as he grabbed her, Courtney faced him. "Rick, sweetie. I think you've been mistaken. I've had a thing for you a long time, too. I just didn't think you had any feelings toward me." She rubbed up against his body, running her hands down the length of him, touching his gun briefly but not making any quick movements to take it.

"Ah ha. I knew it. Get on the cot." He reached down to undo his zipper. She pretended to follow his command and lay down on her back, her legs spread but still fully clothed. She could see the bulge in his underwear as he dropped his trousers. She had to act carefully now. The gun was on the floor, but she couldn't alert Knowles that she was disarming his partner.

Rick removed his shirt. "Now don't be coy, Courtney. It's your turn. Take off your clothes, or do you prefer I undress you?"

She smiled, preparing her attack. "Come here, Rick. I want your hands on me now."

As he slid his naked body onto the cot and leaned forward to grasp a button on her shirt, Courtney jumped up swiftly and put her arms around his neck, placing him in a stranglehold much like one he'd used to kill his disabled victims. "The truth is I find you disgusting," she said. "I'm trained in karate, so I can render you unconscious in two minutes. Enough time to grab that gun you let out of your sight."

She felt him squirming but as she squeezed, his eyes bulged and rolled back. When she was sure he was knocked out, she left him on the cot and seized the gun from his pants pocket. She had to find a way to escape the cabin without Knowles seeing her. There was no way she could make the same move on him. Even the gun might not deter him. Her best bet was to sneak around him. She couldn't think past that. She knew Knowles would spot her on the security camera. If he still wanted her alive, he would go after her. What she really needed to do was disarm the camera, but that would be difficult if Knowles was sitting in front of it.

# Chapter Thirty

Courtney knew Rick wouldn't stay unconscious long. Holding his gun at her side, she gently opened the door and slipped out of the room. As quietly as possible, she moved toward the front of the cabin. Knowles was nowhere in sight. *Where was he? In the bathroom? Outside for a smoke away from the camera's range?*

She tiptoed toward the computer keeping her eyes and ears pealed for any sound of Knowles' approach. When she finally stood before the monitoring device, she pondered how she could disable it. Breaking the screen was out of the question because it would alert Knowles from wherever he was and also possibly awaken Rick. Her only other option was to figure out a way to reprogram it. She stared at the screen. It looked like a simple surveillance camera capturing live feed from the outside around the mountain and the area below it. Could the story Knowles told about it firing at intruders be a ruse, like the bomb? She couldn't bet her life on it, but it made some sort of sick sense like the fact that Rick was killing disabled people to frame Knowles' partner.

She tried to remember some of the computer tricks Bill taught her at Baxter. Rick wasn't the only brother who was adept at technology. She tentatively typed in a sequence that might send the program into a loop and crossed her fingers it would work. But before the screen went blank, something caught her eye on the lower half of the display. The square that captured the street around the mountain showed a four-wheel vehicle. In the early winter darkness, it was hard to make out the car, but she could've sworn it was Bill's. She drew in a breath. If Bill was here, he surely had backup, and how could he even consider scaling the mountain?

She left the computer flashing random numbers and made her way toward the cabin door.

"Just one moment, young lady. Where do you think you're going?" Knowles' voice came from behind her.

She spun around, aiming the gun at him, but his was pointed at her. "I see you didn't like your time with Rick. I don't blame you. He doesn't appeal to me either, but you didn't have to knock him out." He smiled. "No worries. I can handle you myself. Now fix that computer or you'll be sleeping sounder than my partner."

Even if she knew how to remove the loop, Courtney couldn't let Knowles see Bill's car on the monitor. She had to figure a way to stall him and hope that Bill and Sansone's backup men arrived in time.

She lifted her chin and waved her gun. "I will not. You take one step closer, and I'll shoot you."

He seemed to find her threat amusing. "I guess we're at an impasse then. Perhaps Rick can break the tie. I think he'll be waking soon, and he can fix the computer. You won't be able to kill both of us at the same time, and if you shoot me first, Rick will get my gun."

She took a step back toward the PC as if to protect it. She decided to bluff. "The only thing you'll gain from correcting the loop is a few outside pictures. There are no hidden guns in the mountain or around the cabin."

She expected him to deny her words. Instead, his smile widened. "Smart lady. There's no chance anyone will scale that mountain to come to your rescue, anyway. If anyone tries, we'll be long gone by then."

"And how do you suppose to do that without rail tickets?" she asked.

"I have all the fake I.D.'s I need and a jeep behind the cabin. As soon as Rick is up, we'll be departing. I've

changed my mind about using you as collaterol. I don't
think we need to, and you'll just weigh us down."

"And how do you plan to rid yourself of me?" She
was inching closer to the front door, her gun still extended.

He laughed outright. "There are numerous ways
besides shooting you. A good fall over the mountain would
do it. Rick might even strangle you despite the fact you
aren't disabled."

She was only a few feet from the door now. "And
how will you get my gun?"

"No need to get your gun," he said. "because it's
not loaded, my dear. I told Rick to remove the bullets in
case you tried to pull the fast one that you just did. As you
know, I'm the mastermind behind this operation, so I plan
way in advance."

*Was he bluffing? Should she try to shoot him and
then run, or just dash for the door?* It would be difficult to
get down the mountain, but she would have a head start.
Hopefully, Sansone's men or the FBI wouldn't be far away.

She made a split-second decision and bolted,
throwing the door open and running into the chill night.
She heard Knowles' laughter echo behind her. "You won't
get far. I'm trained in mountain climbing, and I so love a
chase."

# Chapter Thirty-One

In the police academy, Courtney had done some climbing drills, but nothing that prepared her for the steepness of the mountainside below the cabin. Just keeping herself steady was a challenge as she inched her way over the rocks. She could hear Knowles' laughter close behind, but then she heard something else—the sound of rocks shifting. She risked losing her grip as she glanced down. The sight below both relieved and frightened her. Mark was attempting to scale the mountain, Bill looked on from the ground, his gun drawn to cover Mark.

Courtney had to find a way to warn the men without alerting the armed Knowles. Hopefully, their backup would be there soon. While she was trying to form a plan, she hesitated too long. Knowles came up behind and grabbed her, knocking the gun out of her hand and sending it sliding down the mountain to rest on a rock close to the bottom. "I told you I was an expert mountain climber. I also see your crazy boyfriends have come to your aid. Too bad. Farrell will never make it up here." With one hand holding her against him, he fired down at Mark who was struggling upward.

The bullet came very close to hitting him. She couldn't let Knowles fire another round. But before she could react, matters got even worse as Rick appeared in the cabin's doorway, his clothes askew from dressing quickly. Assessing the situation, he ambled down to her and Knowles, grabbed her as his partner happily handed her over so that his hands would be free to allow him an even better shot at Mark.

"About time you woke up," Knowles muttered. "Just in time to see me knock off Ms. Lang's buddies down there. Maybe you'll even get another chance with her in the sack before she joins them."

"I don't care about that anymore," Rick said, squeezing her against him. "We need to split, so just finish this job, so we can get away."

"Who's giving orders now, you little runt?" Knowles countered as he turned the gun on Rick and shot him, narrowly missing his heart. Courtney almost fell forward but managed to break free and catch herself.

Rick's eyes bulged in disbelief as he clutched his chest and fell backwards, crashing down toward Bill.

"I planned to do that, anyway," Knowles explained his action. "Now, after I finish the rest of you, I'll have all the money and my revenge for my sister's death." He turned to look down where Rick's body lay below. "I think I'll save you for last, though." As he pointed his gun toward Mark who had stopped climbing when he'd seen the body fall, Courtney knew she had to make a move. She prepared to throw herself at Knowles to knock him down, but he must've sensed her thought because he turned back before she stepped forward.

"Okay then. Change of plans. You're next."

She was stuck with a boulder at her back and nowhere to go but down. The gun was pointed directly at her, and she knew Knowles wouldn't miss. Just as she was about to give up hope, a shot rang out from below. It hit Knowles in the leg, and he staggered forward and fell. She watched as he rolled to the bottom. Finding the strength she thought she'd lost, she scurried down toward Mark. They met on a ledge where he embraced her, wiping tears from her eyes as he hugged her tight. "It's all over," he murmured. "You're safe, thank God."

When Mark released her, she saw Bill below, his service revolver still trained on Knowles. So it was he who had brought Knowles down. The look on Bill's face just dared Knowles to try something.

Knowles just watched him with angry eyes and didn't budge.

# Chapter Thirty-Two

It wasn't long before police swarmed the area. To protect Courtney, Mark had kept them away until she was safe. He signalled them as soon as he had helped her down the mountain. Bill rolled over to Rick whose blood drained from his chest wound onto the rocks around him. Along with the lethal shot, he must've broken bones on the way down. Despite the pain, he looked up at his brother and tried to talk. "You gave me a chance, and I screwed it up, didn't I?" he asked, his voice cracking.

"Yes, Rick," Bill said. "I can forgive you for what you did to me, but not the others. You let drugs and an evil man control you. You could've been so much more." Courtney caught a tear at the side of his eye as Rick took a last breath and lay still.

The police had gotten Knowles down too. An officer had already cuffed him, and a paramedic was standing by to take him to the hospital where he'd be treated before being handed over to the custody of the police. He had no words for them, but the look he gave as he was loaded onto a stretcher was one of pure hate.

Courtney shuddered at the intensity of it, as Mark held her close. Then she heard Sansone's voice through the audio mike clipped to his shirt. "Good job, Detectives."

Bill, still gazing down at his brother, smiled weakly. Mark patted him on the back. "The captain considers this a joint effort, but you were the one who saved the day. I'm proud of you, buddy."

\*\*\*

Knowles was sentenced to theft, several counts of manslaughter, attempted murder, and murder. He was going away for a long time.

Courtney sat at her desk, looking over at the two men sitting side by side across from her. She was glad they had finally worked out their differences and now seemed the best of friends.

"Is it true that Sansone is teaming you back up with Courtney on a permanent basis?" Mark asked Bill.

Bill nodded and smiled, the first happy expression he'd made since Rick's death. "That's partially true. It seems Sansone wants the three of us to work together, and I'm being allowed at some of the crime scenes, too."

"Glad to have you with us," Mark said. "We should all go out and celebrate our new threesome."

Courtney knew Mark had his concerns about Bill, as did she. Sansone's decision would help him stay busy and start to put his brother's deception behind him. But, like the guilt she still carried over her family's fire, she knew Bill felt responsible for not keeping Rick on the straight road.

"I think I'll take a pass," Bill said, "but why don't you two go without me?"

Courtney was pleased when Mark said, "No way, partner. You're coming with us if I have to drag you."

Bill laughed. "I'd better not argue with that."

\*\*\*

Instead of going out to a restaurant, Courtney insisted on inviting the men to dinner at her place. Oliver seemed glad to see them and greeted Mark by rubbing up against his ankle and purring. After receiving a few pats on his head, he ambled over to Bill's chair and sideswiped a wheel. "Careful there, little guy," Bill said.

Courtney reached down and picked up Oliver, gently placing him on Bill's lap where the cat, still purring, snuggled.

"I think he missed both of you," she said. "Have a seat while I prepare your meals, and I don't want either of you to help me."

"You heard the lady," Mark said, sitting on the couch.

While Courtney was in the kitchen tossing a salad and heating the stove top for the steaks that she'd marinated with herbs, she heard the men talking from the other room.

"I'm glad she chose you," Bill said. "I think I knew in my heart when I asked her to marry me last year that she would've turned me down. You can't make someone love you."

"That's true, but I think you'll find the right person for you one day. You're a great guy. I see that now that I've let go of my jealousy."

"Thanks, but I doubt someone would be interested in a cripple."

"You are far more than a cripple, my friend, and there are women who will recognize that. Believe me."

Courtney was touched by Mark's statement. It was then that she thought of Meaghan and decided to see if she was home and would like to join them. She was glad when her neighbor answered and said she was free and would love to stop by for dinner because, after working some long shifts at the hospital, she hadn't had time to grocery shop.

A few minutes later, after Oliver had scurried off of Bill to parts unkown, Meaghan appeared at the door with a bottle of wine, and the rest of the evening turned out nicely. While Meaghan knew both Mark and Bill, Courtney noticed a change in the way her neighbor regarded Bill. She also spotted the special glances Bill threw Meaghan's way as they laughed at jokes together and hoped it was a sign that her matchmaking might work. Both of them deserved the same happiness she was sharing with Mark.

Throughout the night, Mark smiled at Courtney and took her hand. Although she loved the company, she was looking forward to when Bill and Meaghan would leave, and they could have some private moments.

When Bill began to yawn and Meaghan started saying she had an early day at the hospital the next morning, Courtney saw them out. When she returned, Mark was on the couch next to Oliver who had reappeared as the voices had died down.

"I think this guy is glad we're finally alone," he said.

"Not as much as I am." She gently slid the cat off the seat and sat next to Mark. "Do you think Bill and Meaghan will hook up?"

He smiled. "If you have any say in it. They're both good people."

"Yes." She lay her head on his shoulder and sighed. "They both need someone."

"Everybody needs someone. Now come here because I need you." He turned and kissed her, a deep heart hammering kiss that took her breath away.

When she was able to come up for air, she asked, "I guess that means you're staying tonight."

He laughed. "I'm staying forever."

# Epilogue

It was Courtney's idea to hold a memorial service for the victims of the Handicapped Strangler in the spring, four months after Rick's funeral. Mark accompanied her, and Bill was there with Meaghan and Rufus. The dog had also attended his master's funeral. He lay obediently by Bill's wheelchair in a sunny spot of Baxter Park where the service was taking place.

While Rick's home had been restored after the fire, Meaghan had offered to let Bill stay at her place with Rufus until he could find a place of his own. That temporary move became permanent as the two developed a relationship beyond friendship.

Courtney sat between Mark and Meaghan on the chairs set up near the gazebo. Bill sat next to Meaghan. The opposite side of the row was full of officers. Sansone occupied the seat at the end. She wore a black suit. Myra, also in black, sat next to her. Courtney, Mark, and Bill had spent several sessions talking with the staff psychologist after Courtney's rescue.

The family of the victims took up the row in front of the Baxter officers. Edna Black was there with Chirpy perched on her shoulder. The bird was as quiet as Rufus. Edna was wiping her eyes with a handkerchief. Next to her were Mrs. Fredericks and her husband. It seemed to Courtney that Gloria's mother had not stopped crying since she and Mark had spoken with her a few weeks ago. Her husband sat straight up in the chair, gazing forward as if in a trance. Courtney imagined he was sadder than his wife. On the end were students from Baxter U—Winchester Palmer, Sally Collins, Steve Willis, and even Dean Clark sat among coeds who were paying their respects to the memory of their lost, fellow undergrad.

The minister, a thin, balding man in his sixties, greeted everyone and thanked them for coming. "We are here to honor the memories of Agnes McCarver, Joseph Hamilton, and Gloria Fredericks," he began. "Their lives were cut short by an act of violence, but their memories will live on in the hearts of their loved ones. Despite their disabilities, each of them lived their short life fully." He looked across at his audience. "I invite any friend or member of any of the deceased to step forward and say some words about them."

Edna, gripping her handkerchief, stood up and walked to the minister. She still carried Chirpy. "My sister was a wonderful woman," she said between sobs, the bird bouncing gently on her shoulder. "For many years I blamed myself for the accident that blinded her, but I realized that what they say is true, God only gives us burdens we can manage. Aggie was stronger than I could ever be. She never let anything get in her way. I miss her dearly and know she is looking down at me and Chirpy and watching over us. That gives me the strength to go on without her." She blew her nose into the handkerchief, bowed her head, and went back to her chair.

The next person to stand and address the group was Ronald Fredericks. He cleared his throat before he began and loosened the tie at his neck. Courtney thought he resembled a preacher about to speak to his congregation. "I'm here today with others who have lost loved ones in this tragedy," he began. "My daughter, my beautiful Gloria, perished at the hands of a very sick man." He looked toward Bill. "I don't hold any members of his family responsible. A man answers only to himself and to God. My sweet daughter suffered while she was on this Earth, having lost the use of her right arm. Still, she managed to play the piano. She loved music, and I'm sure she's up there in heaven playing a concerto for the angels." He wiped a tear from his eyes and went back to join his wife who had looked up briefly from her handkerchief as he put his arm around her.

As soon as Fredericks was back in his seat, Steve Willis took his place before those gathered at the memorial. "I'm Steve Willis, Joe Hamilton's roommate," he introduced himself. Unlike Gloria's father, Courtney could tell he wasn't a practiced speaker. His hands shook as he took a folded looseleaf sheet from his pocket and opened it. "I wrote a few things I wanted to say about my friend, Joe." His voice began to break as he read: "Joe was my roommate, but he was more than that. He was smart. He was kind. He couldn't hear, but that never stopped him. He made everyone a friend, and I was proud to know him."

He paused and looked toward the group of Baxter attendees. "After it happened, I wished it had been me and not him, but now I realize Joe wouldn't have wanted that. He'd want me to go on with my life and live it to the fullest." His voice began to rise as tears started to roll down his cheeks. "The man who did this, who chose to kill three disabled people, was the one with the biggest disability. God rest his sick soul."

The minister walked over to Steve and touched his arm. "Thank you, Mr. Willis." When Steve had retaken his seat, the minister asked, "Is there anyone else who'd like to speak before I finish this service?"

Bill whispered to Meaghan, "Can you watch, Rufus? I want to go up." Meaghan nodded, and he handed her the dog's leash. Then he rolled himself toward the minister. "I'd like to add a few things, Reverend."

"Surely, Mr. Thompson." The man backed away to give him room.

"You all know my brother was the one responsible for taking the lives of your loved ones and for crippling

211 • Reason to Die

me," he began. "I don't defend his memory or what he did, but there was another man involved, a rich man who took advantage of a misguided young man. Jonathan Knowles is now in prison for his crimes. He will serve a very long time. I know that doesn't bring any of you peace. There are many misjustices in the world. When I was shot, I thought I'd never adjust to being a cripple. I didn't cope as well as Agnes, Joe, or Gloria. I made my handicap an excuse. I should've seen the evil in my brother, the drugs that polluted his mind. That's all in the past now, though. I can't bring back the lives he's taken, but I can continue to devote my life to the law. I thank my fellow officers," he glanced toward Courtney and then Sansone, "and my Captain, for believing in me and treating me as an equal despite my handicap." He then looked toward Meaghan. "Although I've lost the use of my legs and deeply regret the terrible grief my brother and his partner caused all of you, more than ever, I have a reason to live."

There was clapping as he moved back to his spot. Chirpy let out a squawk as if in agreement, and Rufus padded over to him as Bill again took his place by Meaghan. She took his hand in hers, and Courtney's heart leaped at the look of love that passed between them, so similar to the expression in Mark's eyes as he glanced over at her. *Some stories have a happy ending, she thought, even if they take a while to get there.*

# About Debbie De Lousie

Debbie De Louise is an award-winning author and a reference librarian at a public library on Long Island. She is a member of International Thriller Writers, Sisters-in-Crime, the Long Island Authors Group, and the Cat Writer's Association. She has a BA in English and an MLS in Library Science from Long Island University. Her novels include the three books of the Cobble Cove cozy mystery series published by Solstice Publishing: *A Stone's Throw*, *Between a Rock and a Hard Place,* and Written in Stone. Debbie has also published a romantic comedy novella featuring a jewel heist caper, *When Jack Trumps Ace,* and has written articles and short stories for several anthologies of various genres. She lives on Long Island with her husband, Anthony, daughter, Holly, and cat, Stripey.

**Social Media**

Facebook: https://www.facebook.com/debbie.delouise.author/

Twitter: https://twitter.com/Deblibrarian

Goodreads: https://www.goodreads.com/author/show/2750133.Debbie_De_Louise

Linkedin: https://www.linkedin.com/in/debbiedelouise

Amazon Author Page: http://amzn.to/2bIHdaQ

Website/Blog/Newsletter Sign-Up: https://debbiedelouise.com

## Acknowledgements

I'd like to thank the fine staff at Solstice Publishing especially Kathi Sprayberry, Melissa Miller, and Kate Collins for all their hard work on behalf of their authors. They are truly an amazing publisher, and I am very lucky to be part of this group. I'd also like to thank Kelly Abell of Select-o-Grafix, LLC for the beautiful cover she designed.

I would also like to acknowledge my fellow Solstice authors and other author friends as well as my family and all those who have supported me on my publishing journey.

To my newsletter subscribers who entered and won my character naming contest last May, thanks for providing the great monikers for Jonathan Knowles (Lisa Diaz Myers); Harrison Shride (Kathy LeJeune); Carol White (Lisa LaRochell-Davis); and Meaghan Mitchell (Jeri Dickinson).

Last but not least, I give my heartfelt thanks to my readers for their interest and encouragement. I love writing for all of you. Thanks for reading.

# If you enjoyed this story, check out these other Solstice Publishing books by Debbie De Louise:

## A Stone's Throw (Cobble Cove Mystery #1)

**Widowed librarian Alicia Fairmont needs answers...**
After her husband is killed in a hit and run accident, Alicia travels upstate to his hometown of Cobble Cove, New York, hoping to locate his estranged family and shed light on his mysterious past. Anticipating staying only a weekend, her visit is extended when she accepts a job at the town's library.

**Secrets stretch decades into the past...**

Assisted by handsome newspaper publisher and aspiring novelist, John McKinney, Alicia discovers a connection between her absent in-laws and a secret John's father has kept for over sixty years. But her investigation is interrupted when she receives word her house has burned and arson is suspected, sending her rushing back to Long Island, accompanied by John.

**Back in Cobble Cove, cryptic clues are uncovered...**

When Alicia returns, she finds a strange diary, confiscated letters, and a digital audio device containing a recording made the day her husband was killed. Anonymous notes warn Alicia to leave town, but she can't turn her back on the mystery—or her attraction to John. As the pieces begin to fall into place, evidence points to John's involvement in her husband's accident. The past and present threaten to collide, and Alicia confronts her fears…

**Has she fallen in love with her husband's killer?**

myBook.to/Stonesthrow2

**Between a Rock and a Hard Place (Cobble Cove Mystery #2)**

Librarian Alicia McKinney has put the past behind her…

Two years ago, Alicia discovered both a terrible truth and lasting love with John McKinney in the small town of Cobble Cove, New York. Now a busy mother of twin babies and co-author of a mystery series, Alicia couldn't be happier.

Alicia's contentment and safety are challenged…

Walking home alone from the library, Alicia senses someone following her, and on more than one occasion, she believes she is being watched. Does she have a stalker? When the local gift shop is burglarized, the troubling event causes unrest among Alicia and the residents of the quiet town.

John and Alicia receive an offer they can't refuse…

When John's sister offers to babysit while she and John take a much-needed vacation in New York City, Alicia is reluctant to leave her children because of the disturbances in Cobble Cove. John assures her the town is safe in the hands of Sheriff-elect Ramsay. Although Alicia's experience with and dislike of the former Long Island detective don't alleviate her concern, she and John take their trip.

Alicia        faces        her        worst        nightmare…

The McKinneys' vacation is cut short when they learn their babies have been kidnapped and John's sister shot. Alicia and John's situation puts them between a rock and a hard place when the main suspect is found dead before the ransom is paid. In order to save their children, the McKinneys race against the clock to solve a mystery more puzzling than those found in their own books. Can they do it before time runs out?

myBook.to/CobbleCove2

## Written in Stone (Cobble Cove Mystery #3)

Alicia      McKinney      is      confused    .      .      .      .

Was the strange email her husband received from the fictional detective in their mystery series a threat? Did the killer mistake the woman shot in the library for Alicia or the victim's twin sister?

Cat vs. Dog . . .

After Sneaky goes missing from the library, will he turn up before a young girl becomes ill with worry over his disappearance? And will he return in time to outsmart Fido by being first to find the perpetrator's smoking gun?

Alicia is worried . . .

While waiting for the killer's next move, Alicia has other concerns. An old flame of John's is in town and her friend,

Gilly, has adopted the role of Miss Marple to aid her sheriff boyfriend in his investigation.

When all clues point to one of her co-workers, Alicia joins Gilly in searching for the answers to the mystery.

Will they survive . . . .

myBook.to/CC3ebook

**When Jack Trumps Ace**

**Jackie Riordan's in trouble . . .**

When her jewel-thief father is caught in the middle of a heist, Jackie makes her getaway to his ex-jail pal's apartment. a man called Ace, who lives in an upscale neighborhood of Chicago. What she doesn't count on is falling in love with him and becoming his partner in crime. She also doesn't expect to compete with Ace's old flame or deal with his cat Roxie who causes her allergy attacks.

**All bets are off . . .**

After Jackie discovers clues left by her father which lead her to a treasure that Ace may have stolen, she contemplates her next move. Should she trust Ace and believe her father gave him the money, or head home to her mother, a religious hypocrite who would have no qualms about ratting out her own daughter to the cops?

**Things that sparkle aren't always Diamonds . . .**

Before Jackie can decide who the good guys really are, she finds herself atop the Willis Tower carrying her father's ashes in her pocket and aiding Ace in the largest jewelry heist of his life. Things go terribly wrong, and Jackie's only choice seems to be to walk away from Ace or face imprisonment.

myBook.to/Jackebook

**Dying for a Vacation**

When Murder is on the Itinerary

Awaiting his eminent retirement, Detective Donald Jackson plans a much-needed vacation. Before he leaves, he needs to finish writing instructions for his catsitter. More importantly, he has to wrap up a case at the Flower Hill Public Library involving the murder of librarian Phyllis Frost who was poisoned during her coffee break. Returning to the library for another round of suspect questioning, Jackson is not sure he will be able to solve the crime. He only hopes it doesn't delay his trip.

myBook.to/dyingvacation